SOMETHING'S AMISS

DAVE BENNEMAN

For John,

Remember when things are
going well, there is always
Something's Amiss

CELTIC
MOON
PRESS

Copyright © 2018 by Dave Benneman

All rights reserved.

Something's Amiss

Celtic Moon Press

ISBN: 978-1-948884-15-0 (ebook)

ISBN-13: 978-1-948884-14-3 (paperback)

Cover Art: Caleb Benna

Readers are talking...

"An unsettling, mind-bending collection of short stories guaranteed to haunt your waking hours and keep your heart racing..." —Jami Gray, Author of Kyn Kronicles, Fate's Vultures, & PSY-IV Teams

"This collection of short stories was such a refreshing change from a lot of books out there in the same genre. Every story was very different, yet they fit together seamlessly in consumable little bites of horror. Dave Benneman did a great job at creating well thought out, complex characters and putting them in situations that really suck the reader in. Most of the stories left me guessing how they would end, and I was never disappointed. Do yourself a favor and pick up Something's Amiss for a good book you can really immerse yourself in. I highly look forward to the next book." —Neila F., Red Adept Editing

Also by Dave Benneman

Drowning in Darkness

For Edgar Allen Poe
The first in a long line of short fiction writers who captured my soul in the crucible of imagination.

Contents

Introduction

Welcome, intrepid visitors, to the inner workings of a twisted mind.

What you hold in your hand is a collection of twelve stories I felt were worthy of your time. Some may scare you or leave you unsettled. Maybe you will encounter an unexpected twist that defies your reality.

I hope your journey into my dominion is not altogether unpleasant.

Thank you.
db

A Picture Is Worth A Thousand Screams

P hil guzzled half a bottle of water before surveying his surroundings. The desolate section of dunes between the old coast road and the Pacific Ocean ensured zero possibility of light pollution. The march across a half mile of windswept dunes while carrying his photography equipment had proven to be tougher than he'd expected. Tall dune grass surrounded him, providing the foreground he'd imagined when he'd decided to document the rising of the largest super moon of the decade.

Carefully, he spread out a small blanket over the sand, on which to lay his camera bag. The tripod legs sank into the dune, giving it a sturdy base upon which he mounted his most recent acquisition. The massive lens had set him back a small fortune. Next, he programmed the custom settings mode on his Nikon, which would provide him with instant access to a variety of aperture settings and timed exposures. A glance at his watch confirmed the moon's imminent arrival. He closed the camera bag and set it out of the way.

The full moon edged above the horizon, evicting the

sun from the sky. Phil continually made minute adjustments to capture the moon as it peered through the dune grass. The wind stilled, and the scene became eerily quiet. The distant surf provided a muffled soundtrack. They called it a blood moon, but in truth, it was orange-yellow. The light cast an otherworldly feel to the familiar surroundings of sand, surf, and grass. Phil shook off the sense that he was being watched. Only the moon was in a position to watch him.

Once the moon hung aloft in a predominantly clear sky, his attention drifted. He fancied himself a visual composer. Instead of lining up musical notes to play a coherent melody, he arranged and captured fragments in each frame to create complex images. Next, his role was relegated to that of a roadie. It was time to pack up and haul his equipment out of there. The decision to lug his gear across a half mile of sweeping dunes for the shot now seemed questionable. Thousands of cameras around the world were filming the same event.

A dark cloud appeared from nowhere, obliterated the starlight, and pushed a spearhead across the face of the moon. The monstrously large orange circle now wore an interesting detail. Its shattered reflection played on the surface of the Pacific. This gave his subject an appealing feature, appealing enough to photograph. With his attention back on the view screen, Phil clicked the wireless remote for each exposure.

The wind kicked up and sang a discordant tune. It carried a pungent smell under the fresh ocean scent. The sand hissed as it sailed through the tall grass. Something moved in his peripheral vision. He remained riveted to the spectacle overhead. The spearhead blunted, and the moon gradually disappeared. He held his breath. The perfect fingernail crescent photograph approached the threshold. He took a rapid blast of photos just as the lights went out.

"I'm such an idiot!" His gadget bag lay a minor ten to twelve feet away with fabulous sources of artificial light, but in this cave-like darkness, it might as well have been miles. Once the moon and stars were blanketed, he lost all reference of time and space. The deep sand and tall grass were difficult to move through in full sun. In total darkness, he feared falling on his face or, worse yet, breaking an ankle. He waited, frozen to the spot, knowing the cloud cover would pass.

A whispering sound filled his head. Something moved through the grass—a lot of somethings. The movement didn't sound like the clumsy way a person stumbled around. This was lithe, graceful, and delicate. It came from everywhere and nowhere, which unsettled Phil.

The dark held sway, and the sounds were foreign to him. The funky odor intensified. Sweat beaded on his forehead in spite of the October breeze blowing off the Pacific. He waited. The impulsive side of Phil wanted to search for his gear bag, but cautious Phil said, "Be quiet, asshole, or we'll be stuck here all night with a sprained ankle."

Reckless Phil: "Do something, you pansy."

Cautious Phil: "Doing nothing is doing something."

Reckless Phil was not equipped to have an argument that employed logic. Round two went to Cautious Phil on points.

The sound moved toward the ocean like a thousand single blades of dune grass slithering through the sand. The edge of the cloud took on an orange glow. The moon struggled to be seen. Phil's eyes, which had become accustomed to the complete darkness, could make out shapes. With the promise of impending light, he felt around for his equipment bag. Movement on the beach caught his attention. Hundreds of creatures moved about like a modern dance troop. They were long and lithe, like bundles of vines. Segments moved out to their sides, much like dancers used their arms.

The orange glow cast shadows around them, making it difficult to discern shadow from dancer. "Beautiful," he whispered. "Camera, idiot."

Phil repositioned his camera and started taking photos. He felt like a voyeur stealing images of a private ballet like an unscrupulous paparazzo. Instinctively, he knew he shouldn't be photographing the scene. His intrusion, if discovered, would send these creatures running for cover, spoiling the spectacle. The camera clicked and whirred anyway.

Urgency harassed him. With no way of knowing how long the phenomenon would continue, he rushed his normal careful compositions. His hands fluttered over the camera controls, making adjustments. He captured the whole group in some shots and close-ups in others.

A blurry shape moved across his lens. The moon shone a little brighter. Phil glanced up. One of the creatures leaned over him. It was reedy, over six feet tall, and slender, like a bunch of entwined roots. Fine sand clung to it, glistening in the moonlight. It had no distinct head, arms, legs, or face. Still, it seemed to be looking into the lens inquisitively. Phil's heartbeat thudded in his ears, drowning out every other sound.

With a sharp intake of breath, he clicked the camera, and the creature slithered into the sand as if it were standing on a cloud instead of terra firma.

Relief flooded through Phil. "I guess I'll be going now."

Intuitively, he understood he'd overstayed his welcome. He slung the tripod over his shoulder and took a step toward the gadget bag. His foot sank deeply into the sand. His second step was awkward, and he descended deeper still. He struggled for balance. Something twined around his legs and tugged at his ankles. He tossed the tripod away and seized the dune grass, uprooting and tossing handfuls of it aside for a fresh hold. He fought heroically, pulling and ripping to keep himself from descending farther. His legs kicked hard at the creature that pulled him down.

He struggled for breath as he battled for his life. He bellowed with rage until his mouth filled with sand, muffling his final scream.

The only witness to Phil's demise was his Nikon, which lay a few feet away, slowly disappearing under the drifting sand.

Juggling Time

_____

Guy Lafitte dropped his duffle bag at his feet. The sun touched the ocean, playing out act one of the daily drama that attracted tourists to Monti's Pier. The hive response of one collective *ah* amounted to a stage manager's announcement of *two minutes to show time*. He laid a length of rope on the weathered boards, outlining his piece of the pier.

In the space next to his, Anita stroked her performers with whispers of encouragement. She'd made herself up to look like a mouse, complete with ears and whiskers. The Mighty Mouseketeers, Anita's trained mice, dazzled kids and adults alike with feats of strength and agility. Guy understood all too well how mice could be trained to perform tricks.

He hung his modest banner, a former pillowcase with **DEFYING GRAVITY** painted in dayglow orange, then set out his clubs in a neat line. The appreciative crowd erupted into spontaneous applause that drifted on the sea breeze, which signified the sun had dipped below the horizon. The tourists, customers, or marks, depending on a person's point of view, would soon be strolling the gauntlet of food venders, souvenir peddlers, and street performers.

The competition among the entertainers was fierce but friendly. Volcano Joe spat jets of fire into the air, lighting up the twilight. Joe was a big crowd pleaser. Malcolm the Magnificent performed card tricks and other forms of prestidigitation. A pretty young lady took money from mostly young men with her version of the shell game. Across the pier, the Greek perspired over a grill filled with Italian sausage, onions, and peppers. Gulls squawked overhead, incited by the aroma of grilled meat surfing the salt air.

With more than a little finesse, Guy flipped his top hat into the air. It soared end over end until it landed upside down at the edge of his space, inviting passersby to fill it with dollars. He surveyed the crowd carefully to see if anyone had noticed. One young boy was intrigued enough to pull his mother to a halt.

With no fanfare, Guy selected three clubs and spun them into the air.

Two little girls with ice cream dripping over their fingers joined their mom and big brother. Dad trailed behind, clutching a fistful of napkins. Guy had the beginnings of an audience.

With a finger alongside his jaw, he sighed loud enough to be heard over the other hawkers and performers. "I seem to have forgotten something." He continued spinning the three clubs through the air, taking his time to scratch his head. "Ah yes, music."

He pulled a phone from his pocket and thumbed the buttons as if he'd forgotten the clubs completely. A small Bluetooth speaker came to life behind him. Queen led his play list with "We Will Rock You." He was back in time to save the forgotten objects from hitting the ground. A smattering of applause drew the attention of two young couples. He took a long drink from a water bottle, all the while keeping the clubs spinning with one hand.

The bluest eyes he'd ever seen stared into his soul over a single scoop of chocolate.

"How many clubs are there?" he asked her.

Ice cream graced her dimpled chin as she stared over his head.

Her brother started to butt in, but Guy silenced him with a look. "Let her answer."

"One blue, one red, one yellow. Three!" she cried in triumph.

"That's right." He applauded her. "Three is so yesterday, right?"

She nodded solemnly. Chocolate ran down her arm and dripped from her elbow, unnoticed.

"Let's do five." He picked up two and added them to the blur of color swirling overhead. His boom box shifted into "Dirty Deeds Done Dirt Cheap." This time, the applause was greater, and now his audience stood two and three deep in places. A modest collection of greenbacks accumulated in his hat.

"How many now?" He nodded to the little boy this time.

"Five." As the word left the child's lips, Guy kicked another club into the air. "Six now," the boy corrected just as Guy's foot lifted another club into the rotation.

"How many?" Guy teased.

"Seven!"

The cookie lady pedaled slowly by, hawking her home-baked delights from her tricycle. Guy maintained seven clubs while he engaged the folks who walked past without a glance, firing off his litany of nonsense. "Hey. Where you going? It doesn't cost anything to look." An older white-haired woman strolled along. Guy caught her attention. "Hey, beautiful, what are you doing later? Want to go dancing?"

She smiled and shook her head.

Guy sharpened his focus. He used his true talent to slow time. Only a little, but enough to kick another club into the air.

The crowd joined the boy in shouting, "Eight."

A tourist rushed by in a hurry.

"Hey, did Joe set another tourist on fire?" Guy asked.

The Animals sang "We Gotta Get Out Of This Place," and as if on cue, a couple in the crowd elbowed their way out.

"Don't leave before the magic happens," Guy called. "At least hang around until I drop some of these."

Around Guy, time shifted again. It did so unnoticed, or so he believed. For him, the clubs traveled through syrup instead of air. The noise of the pier sounded like a tape slowing down.

"Nine!" The crowd exploded with whistles and cheers. His audience grew, blocking the thoroughfare. The curious were drawn by the growing crowd. Color soared high above his head.

A panhandler, new to the pier, left his cup of spare change and walked slowly toward the excitement.

"Ten!" Sweat dripped from Guy's face. His shirt clung to him.

The panhandler inched closer, staring intently.

"Eleven!"

Fatigue caressed Guy's limbs. The weight of time sapped his strength. His arms became sluggish.

"Twelve!"

"What do you say we wrap this up?" The strain of keeping the blur over his head in motion instead of clattering to the ground embraced him. He kicked the final club into the air.

"Thirteen!" the crowd yelled.

"A baker's dozen." Aretha Franklin asked for a little "Respect" from his boom box. The panhandler's steely gaze distracted Guy's concentration. He struggled to keep the impossible number of clubs spinning a minute more. This was the moment everyone waited for with an expectation that the clubs would come clattering to the ground at any second. The crowd sang along with the queen of soul, R-E-S-P-E-C-T. Guy took his cue to bring it home. He caught one club and slipped it into his gear bag. The young boy who was first to arrive at his show counted backward, while the crowd continued to sing. "Twelve."

"Eleven."

The deadbeats stealthily slipped away from the press of the crowd. "Ten."

"Nine."

"Eight."

In the exodus, Guy lost sight of the overtly curious homeless man from earlier.

"Seven."

"Six."

He stowed each club safely in his duffle.

"Five."

"Four."

The last three came in together. "Three, two, one."

Pink Floyd launched into "Money." Bowing, Guy picked up his hat and thrust it into the dissipating crowd, singing along with David Gilmore. "Thank you. Thank you." He made eye contact with every person who made a deposit. "Same time tomorrow. A whole new act. Defying Gravity performs nightly at Monti's Pier. Tell your friends."

His very first customer was still there, a bouquet of bills blossoming in his hand.

Guy knelt down so he was eye level with the boy. "Did you enjoy the show?"

"Yeah. You were great."

"You're too kind." Guy felt the panhandler watching him again. A warning flare burst into bright life in the pit of his stomach. "Is all that for me?"

The boy nodded. "Thirteen dollars. One for each thing." He thrust the money toward Guy. "My dad said that's fair."

"Thank you." Guy shook the young man's hand as he looked around to find the dad watching. "That's very generous. Will you thank your dad for me?"

"Okay." The boy spun away and joined his family. The mom was busy trying to unsticky his sister's fingers.

Guy's playlist arrived at the final song, and Bruce Springsteen sang "Born to Run." "That's my cue to get a move on myself." He grabbed his rope, stuffed the money from his hat into a pocket, and shouldered his bag. With each move, he stole another look at the beggar.

Clear, steady eyes watched Guy's every move—the first clue that this man was not what he appeared. Clean finger-nails were the second clue, and all Guy needed. He had to get out of there. Pronto.

With the bag on his shoulder, he zigzagged between cars across the dim parking lot. His breath came in ragged gasps. *How did they find me again?* He doubled back, crouched between two cars, and listened so hard for foot-steps that his ears hurt. He hoped to make enough money working off the grid to make a run to the Pacific North-west. It was rumored that one could disappear in cities like Portland or Seattle.

He chanced raising his head enough to look around.

The area remained clear. He backed over to a rusted white van. It had no windows in the back, providing Guy with the privacy he needed to live in it. The side door screeched as Guy opened it. Then he jumped in behind his bag and closed the door. He took a minute to calm himself then clambered over his bedding. Crouched slightly behind and between the seats, he watched the mirrors on both sides.

In the left mirror, he watched the vagrant walking along the side of the van, looking in every direction. The man spoke into a cell phone. "I lost him." He moved directly in front of the van.

The jackhammer in Guy's chest loudly chipped a hole in his rib cage. He slowed his breathing for fear of being heard.

The man turned in a circle like a searchlight. "Nah. He made me."

Guy ducked behind the driver's seat.

"He won't be back. Damn it to hell. We had him." A dark-gray sedan stopped in front of the van, and the imposter beggar slid into the passenger's seat.

Guy would give them time to clear out then head north on Highway One toward Oregon. He made mental plans while his pursuers sat not ten feet in front of him. He scoffed. "If you fools only knew how close you were."

The smell of flowers drifted over him, drowning out the smell of fear-laced sweat that poured off his body. "What are they waiting for?" A sense of dread nagged at his brain as sleep threatened to pull him under. Too late, he realized something was seeping into the van. Light-headed and dizzy, he climbed into the driver's seat and thrust the key in the ignition. Two men approached his van, one on each side. Guy shifted into drive and floored it. The impact with the sedan and the screech of metal were the last things he remembered.

Guy woke in a white room. The sheets draped over him blended with the walls that bled into the ceiling. He blinked, trying to clear his vision. His nose itched, but when he tried to scratch it, he pulled against restraints. He thrashed his arms and legs wildly against the straps then threw his head back and screamed, "No!"

A barely discernible door opened, and a figure in a white lab coat strode in. "Welcome home, Jude."

"Fuck you."

"Fuck you, *Doctor*, if you don't mind."

He clenched his fists, imbedding his fingernails into his palms. "I do mind. I mind like hell."

"Come now, Jude. It's not so bad here, is it? It must be better than living on the street. Your year of freedom drove you to stealing food to survive. Living in a box on a subway grate. Riding the rails like a hobo from the thirties. And finally, living in a van, masquerading as a street performer for chump change."

Jude clenched his jaw and scanned the whiteness, looking for telltale signs of the cameras and microphones he knew must be there.

"We feed you, quite well I might add. You have a comfortable residence. Twenty hours a day, you can do whatever you want. And still, you run away and betray us to the media. Seriously, did you think we wouldn't find you?"

"It took you almost a year." He sneered. "Another month, and I would have been long gone."

"There's no accounting for incompetence, is there? I must say, out of all the clever monikers you adopted to hide from us, I liked Guy Lafitte best. You pronounced it like the French, *oui*?" The doctor moved to the foot of the bed. "To support your Canadian passport, no doubt. I don't know what you paid, but I think you got ripped off. It would never have gotten you across the border. It was, how you Americans say, cheap imitation, *non*?" She spoke the last line with a heavy French accent.

"What do you want? I'm tired. I need sleep."

"I doubt that very much since you slept like a proverbial baby all the way across the country last night."

Jude started in surprise. "I'm back in Virginia?"

"I'm afraid so." The corners of the doctor's mouth lifted in a humorless bloodred smile. "Sorry to say there will be no more outings after that little show you put on." The slow shake of the doctor's head infuriated Jude. "It's a shame, really. Your fellow students enjoyed getting off campus once in a while."

"Students! You mean lab rats, don't you? Let's cut through the bullshit and call it what it is, shall we, Dr. Stone?"

"There is no need for this animosity between us. If you cooperate, I will get your privileges reinstated. If you don't, you will remain here, staring at white walls all day. It's up to you."

"You're wrong, *Doctor*. It's not up to me. I'm a prisoner whether I'm in restraints or roaming around the residential wing with my fellow rats. Doesn't matter if I'm eating steak or that slop you shove in a feeding tube. As long as I remain here, I'll always be a prisoner."

"I'm sorry you feel that way." Dr. Stone turned on her heel to leave. She paused near the wall, and the door popped open. "I'd hoped we could find some common ground on which to rebuild our relationship."

"Relationship? It takes two to have a relationship. Take off these restraints, you cunt." The door disappeared back into the wall in Dr. Stone's wake. Jude propped himself up on his elbows and directed his comments to the mirror that dominated one wall. "I'm afraid you're delusional, Doctor. You should see a shrink. Ask Dr. Baird what he thinks. He's a team player. He'll tell you what you want to hear." He dropped back down to the mattress. "Another thing. If you think I'm performing for visiting dignitaries, you better think again. Fuck you and your shit French accent." He thought she might return to tell him off, but she didn't. *I'll have to try harder next time.*

In the observation room, Dr. Baird took notes on a legal pad in front of a bank of monitors, on which Jude raged from his bed. *The C word. That's a nice touch.*

Dr. Stone slammed the door open like a linebacker. "Damn it to hell. Why does he have to be so difficult?"

Baird replaced the cap on his fountain pen and turned to face Stone. "Are you asking my professional opinion?"

"Of course I want your professional opinion. That's why I asked you to observe, for Christ's sake."

He took a deep breath and blew it out slowly. Her inability to rattle him drove her crazy. It was one of the few things that gave him joy these days. Irritating Stone had become Baird's pastime in recent months. Stone held Baird responsible for Jude's escape, and she made no attempt to hide her animosity. Once Baird had concluded she would never let up, he'd started his campaign of aggravating her. He crossed one leg over the other and clasped his hands over his knee. "He's very angry."

"You don't need a doctorate in forensic psychology to see that. The guy who cleans the toilets can tell me that. Get with the program, Baird. I need to reach him."

"First, let me say that pointing out his failures and

dismissing his accomplishments while he was on the lam does nothing to alleviate his resentment."

"I know that, but he baits me." Stone paced several steps and stopped. "Did you hear what he called me?"

Baird struggled to suppress a grin. "He feels betrayed. He made that quite clear before he made a run for it. You sold him and his family a bill of goods to get him to sign on for the research. In the interim, he became your prize pupil. His cooperation is the only leverage he has. He's not giving up anything until he gets the respect he feels he deserves."

She ran a hand through her short blond hair. "What the hell does that mean?"

"If you treat him as an equal, let him come and go as you do, afford him the same courtesy a team member would receive—except me of course—maybe, just maybe, you will convince him to participate as a volunteer."

"That's not going to happen."

"No, of course not. Which means he's correct. He *is* your prisoner."

"What does that leave me to work with?"

"Let me dig into some case studies. Maybe there's a way to utilize Stockholm syndrome to convince Jude to be helpful."

"Stockholm syndrome applies to hostages who fear for their lives."

"You don't think he fears for his old life?"

Stone narrowed her eyes.

Baird continued. "The survival instinct is key to Stockholm syndrome. Victims depend on their captors and interpret small acts of kindness in the midst of horrible conditions as good treatment. They often become sensitive to the needs and demands of their captors, linking the captors' survival to their own."

"So I should threaten to kill him if he doesn't comply?"

"It's not that simple. I suggest you try to gain some empathy by being vulnerable. Express the pressure you're under from your superiors. Make them the bad guys. The positive bond between captive and captor is enhanced by a negative attitude toward the authorities that threaten the captor-captive relationship. We need to create a bad guy, a third party whom you both can hate and bond over. Hence, the enemy of my enemy becomes my ally."

Dr. Stone tapped a pen against her bottom lip, a sign the wheels were grinding inside her pretty head. "I'll give that some serious thought."

"I'll create some ways you may be able to manipulate Jude to your side." Baird uncrossed his legs. "Something less brutal than taking him hostage."

"He already thinks of himself as a hostage. All we need is a common enemy as you said."

"Jude is a complicated young man. We have to tread cautiously."

She waved him off. "Thank you, Doctor. I'll handle it from here." Turning her back on him, she stared at Jude through the two-way mirror.

"Dr. Stone." He hesitated, looking for the right phrasing. "I'd like to reiterate my position on Jude's confinement. Let me see him. Maybe I can reach a—"

She spun in the chair to glare at him. "Indeed, because you were so effective last time. I recall that it was your suggestion we allow them to leave the compound. That set us back a year or more."

"At least take off the restraints."

"All in due course, Doctor." She turned back to face the monitor and opened her tablet.

When Baird reached the door, he took a moment to observe Stone's behavior. She pushed herself hard. If she didn't let up, she would crack soon. Silently, he thanked God he was not responsible for her mental stability.

The expensive industrial carpet deadened the sound of his steps as he walked past the magnificent art on loan from the Smithsonian. He no longer saw the art, let alone appreciated it. He'd become jaded to his posh working conditions long ago. The exquisite meals had become as tasteless as his work. Experimenting on young human beings to enhance their unusual abilities was the fodder for science-fiction novels. That didn't stop those in power from speculating. Unlimited funding eliminated any possibility the research would be used for humanitarian reasons. Baird doubted there was a humanitarian within a hundred miles of Langley.

In his plush office, he used his computer to call up the video feed of Jude and muted the sound. Dr. Stone had determined that depriving Jude of stimuli would coerce him into cooperating. In a general sense, that was true enough. However, in his sessions with Jude, Baird had found a young man comfortable in his own company. He interacted with his fellow students, not out of a need for their friendship or approval, but because it would be rude not to. It mattered to him whether others perceived him as rude.

Baird had determined that the best way to reach Jude would be to deprive the others as a consequence of his actions. But he wouldn't share that particular opinion with Stone. She was all too willing to allow these young people to suffer for what she considered the greater good. Aside from lining her pockets and enhancing her résumé, Baird could see no greater good.

Although Baird was kept from visiting Jude, he periodically checked the live video feed from Jude's room while he busied himself with making notes and reviewing the progress of the other students. Jude passed the hours quietly. Aside from some yoga poses, Jude usually sat or lay on his bed, completely still, eyes closed. He seemed to draw into himself. Baird thought he had learned some meditation techniques during his hiatus from the facility.

The eleven other students showed little improvement on the drug cocktail administered by Stone and her group of scientists and neurologists. A young woman who had displayed empathic abilities was inconsistent and showed little if any development. Another young man could solve puzzles and see patterns where no one else could. Yet he was unable to decipher encrypted messages the way they had hoped. The rest continued to backslide after the supposedly enhancing drugs were administered.

Jude had been the only one to respond to the drug regimen. He'd been off them for almost a year. Baird wanted to know if his prowess with manipulating time had diminished. The night they picked him up, Dr. Stone had restarted his daily cocktail of medications immediately.

Baird looked up from his notes. The image of Jude flickered for a moment. He hit the side of the monitor in a reflexive move that never worked for him. "I need a nap." The teakettle would provide a quick lift until he could go home. While the water heated up, he paced back and forth, considering the enigma that was Jude Westin.

All twelve of the young people at the facility were brilliant and had been accepted into Ivy League schools that only the very rich could afford. Even with scholarships, their families had been looking at years of debt. Then Stone and her cronies had arrived to save the day, offering the kids a free college education to any school they chose in exchange for two years of their lives. It was a tempting offer. Jude had been the first to realize what was going on.

He'd planted seeds of mistrust among the others, causing Stone to isolate him.

In high school, Jude had mastered every sport he'd taken an interest in—tennis, baseball, wrestling, and jujitsu. Baird's preliminary workup had indicated that Jude had exceptional hand-eye coordination. Stone's team had tested him to impossible levels. It was Stone who'd discovered what no one else had figured out, including Jude himself. Jude could slow down an action so he had time to react to whatever came his way.

That little observation had moved Stone into the driver's seat of the Research and Development for the Gifted Program—a pretty title for what they were doing, which was tampering with the minds of a dozen young people. If they managed any kind of results, the program would be enlarged, giving Stone the top job with more resources at her disposal. What frightened Baird was the vision of an entire campus of young people whose youth would be sacrificed for some nefarious purpose.

The opinion that the other students would respond when the chemists found the right compound still prevailed among the staff around the facility. As far as Stone was concerned, Jude's refusal to cooperate was the worm in her apple. He represented her most immediate and promising opportunity to demonstrate results. Those results would guarantee the money kept flowing.

Baird decided to call it a day. He dumped out his cup of tea and shut down his computer.

For the last two days, under the cover of sleeping, Jude had been experimenting with his talent. He stretched and staggered into the shower to shake off the drowsiness. Clouds of steam rose, and a hot stream sluiced down his back. A shudder swept through him in spite of the water temperature. *Something changed last night. Stone said I slowed time. I thought she was right about that. It felt right. But last night, time stopped. I slipped out of time. I wasn't in the room anymore. I wasn't anywhere.* He wanted to talk about it, but that wasn't possible.

Stone had removed his restraints on her second visit against the advice of her superiors, or so she'd claimed. He didn't trust her, couldn't trust her.

His stomach growled. *Damn, I'm starving.* He hoped his breakfast would arrive soon. His nocturnal activities raised hell with his internal clock. The arrival of his meals gave him the opportunity to reset it. He lived in the moment. Except when he suspended time. *What the hell is living in the moment when there are no moments?* Because last night, time had stopped. At least it had stopped for him.

The room was bright enough to perform surgery. And they burned twenty-four seven. He could deal with the boredom, but he needed to get the lights off or at least dimmed. That required a change in tactics. *I'm upping the game. I hope Stone gets here soon with my breakfast.* As if on cue, the door clicked, and Stone walked in followed by two large, serious-looking men. Jude supposed they were there to protect her. Why two were needed, he wasn't sure. Either one of them could've broken him in half. He guessed someone had to push the cart with his breakfast. He had dubbed them Spike and Lee.

Stone maintained a neutral zone between them. "Good morning, Jude. Did you sleep well?"

"Actually, I didn't." He rearranged his pillows and sat up straight. "Can we talk for a moment?"

"Of course. What can I do for you?"

He smiled. "If I meet you halfway, will you grant me a few things?"

"Will you allow me to examine you without struggling?"

"Do your thing."

Stone approached him as she would a skittish horse. Spike stayed close.

"May I eat while you work? I'm starving."

"You got your appetite back. That's a good sign." She motioned for Lee to bring his breakfast to the bed. "What is it I can do for you?"

"Can you turn off the lights? I can't sleep." He lifted a bite of an omelet to his mouth. "They mess with my, what's that thing called, arcadia rhythms."

She ran a device across his forehead then documented his temp on a tablet. "You mean your circadian rhythms."

"Yeah, and I'm bored. Can I request some books from the library?"

"Let's not get carried away. Besides, if I dim the lights for you, how will you read?" She moved closer and applied the blood pressure cuff. Spike and Lee moved closer also.

"Maybe a nightstand and a lamp. It would give the place a homey touch."

"I'll adjust the lights for you. We'll see where that leads."

He nodded.

She couldn't conceal the arrogant smirk riding her features. "Left arm, please."

He held out his left arm for her. "Can you get me a book on basic physics?"

She tied off his arm. "Make a fist." After preparing the vials for his blood, she nodded and stuck him. "Why the sudden interest in physics? Weren't you reading that post-apocalyptic stuff before?"

"The first rule of juggling is that no two objects can occupy the same space at the same time. That's physics."

The vials of his blood piled up. "I'll see what I can do. A book on physics will put you to sleep." After pulling the needle from his arm, she consulted her tablet. "Left hip, and we're done."

He rolled over and took a deep breath. The injection stung like a bitch for the first minute.

She passed the tray containing his blood samples to Spike. "Get this to the lab right away."

Jude guzzled the orange juice. "Can you hang for a few minutes?"

"Sure." She dismissed Lee. "So why the sudden change in attitude?"

Jude swallowed and touched a napkin to his mouth. "Not really a change in attitude. I don't like you. I don't respect what you're doing here." He took a bite, making her wait while he chewed. "But what's the point in getting the shit beat out of me every morning for nothing? In the end"—he patted his butt where he received his daily injection—"you get what you want anyway. Pun totally intended."

"I dreaded coming in here with your meals. You've made this easier for everyone involved. Thank you. Maybe my boss will take his boot off my neck now."

"Yeah, well, I'm sorry if I've made your life difficult." He poured himself a coffee from the carafe. "I'd offer you some, but I only have the one cup."

"Will you submit to some testing?"

He stuffed a croissant into his mouth to control his rising anger. *She's unbelievable!* After washing down the pastry with a long drink, he used his napkin again. Finally, he looked into her deep-brown eyes. "To use your words, Doctor, let's not get carried away."

Her hard edges visibly sharpened. "I'll see you at lunch, then."

"Okay. Bring yourself a chair next time, and don't forget the lights. *Please.*"

A couple minutes later, the lights dimmed. He sighed and closed his eyes. In the moments before sleep took him, he contemplated his experience the night before. *Where did I go? What happened to me? If I'm not here, then where am I? It's not an out-of-body thing. I don't think it is, anyway. I didn't see myself. There was no bright light. Actually, there was no light, come to think of it. I need to get into the library. I need—*

"Jude. Wake up, Jude."

Jude rolled over at the touch on his shoulder.

Dr. Stone leaned over him. "Hey, I guess you really did need some rest."

"Hey." He knuckled the sleep from his eyes. "What time is it?"

"It's lunchtime." She took his temperature. Spike and Lee hovered in the background. "Arm, please."

He waited for her to get his blood pressure. "Thanks for turning down the lights."

She motioned to Spike and Lee. Lee set a chair next to Jude, and Spike rolled his lunch over.

"Would you answer a few questions for me?" Stone asked.

Jude started on his salad. "Depends."

"Have you experienced any differences in your health, mental or physical, since you've returned?"

"I'm very tired. I'm not sleeping." He drank some water. "For instance, I could go right back to sleep."

"Are you dreaming? Having nightmares?"

"My turn. Did you find anything on physics for me?"

She smiled. "I did." She pulled a book from the bottom of the cart. *"A Layman's Introduction to Physics."*

He reached for the book. "Great."

Stone kept a grip on it even as she passed it to him. "Dreams?"

"Not that I can remember."

She released her grip. He opened the book and read through the table of contents.

"Jude?"

"Hmm?"

"I know you manipulated time as part of your act. Have you tried since you've returned?"

"You shouldn't get greedy."

"You made it clear you wouldn't participate in any tests. I thought you could at least answer a few questions."

"And I have answered a few." He rolled over and closed his eyes.

She held up a LED book light. "For reading during those sleepless nights." He stretched his hand out for it, but she kept it just out of his reach. "A simple yes or no. Have you been manipulating time since your return?"

Jude used all his reserves to control his anger. He pushed his half-eaten lunch away, slouched down, and turned away. "Sorry I'm not better company. I'm just so tired."

"I'll see you later, then."

He picked his head up and faked a yawn. "I'll be here." *Maybe.* He was tired. He'd slept about five hours, and all he wanted at that moment was to get back there, which was so unlike him. He could normally go full tilt boogie on two hours of sleep. *When I did my act, I was tired right after, but not for a whole day. But I never went that deep.*

He thought about his limited knowledge of energy. *Energy can't be created. You can transfer it, conserve it, and convert it. It makes sense if I exert energy, I have to refuel. When I slipped into that nothingness last night, I must have exerted a lot of energy.*

Previously when he had slowed time, he'd remained present. The same question plagued him. *Where did I go last night? How did I get back?* He picked up the book Stone had brought him and flipped to sections that he hoped might illuminate what had happened. Stone was right about one thing. Physics could be a real snooze-fest, and reading it put him back to sleep.

He woke feeling refreshed. Some of the more abstract theories he'd read in the book before his eyes closed lingered. A multidimensional world was the one that stuck. If he was able to move from one dimension to another, then he should be able to slip right out of the facility. The problem was that he didn't know where he would slip to.

In the place he'd gone, there was no form and no sound. He couldn't even say for sure if he'd stood on anything. *Maybe I dreamt the whole thing.* That morning, he was certain he'd slipped time or dimensions. Now he doubted that anything had happened at all. He needed to get back there, or better yet, go somewhere else. He'd read novels in the past about alternate realities. If he could get to one of those… *That would blow Stone's mind.*

Yesterday, he'd practiced slowing time whenever he wanted, but now he wasn't sure what would happen in his absence. He decided to wait until after dinner.

The lights came on to their full brightness, and the door clicked. Stone pushed in his meal cart and shut the door. "You're looking more refreshed. How do you feel?"

"Much better. Thanks again for dimming the lights." He made an exaggerated point of looking around her. "Where's your entourage?"

"I no longer need them, do I?"

There was a tap on the door. Stone turned and opened it. She pulled in a chair and muttered something Jude couldn't make out. "This is better, isn't it?" She pushed his dinner over to him then pulled the chair up next to his bed.

Jude sat up straight and pulled the cart over to him. "Smells great."

Stone sat. "You're probably hungry. You hardly touched your lunch."

He started on his salad. "Too tired to eat, I guess."

She placed the book light on his tray. "I apologize for this." She nudged it over to him.

"For what?"

"I didn't mean to treat you like a trained dolphin earlier. It was rude and demeaning. I'm sorry. My boss is really pressuring me. That's not an excuse, just an explanation. I'm not myself, because they're riding me."

"Yeah, that"—he motioned to the book light with his fork—"made me mad."

She laughed. "Just a little. Not that anyone noticed the daggers shooting from your eyes. But I understand. So, a peace offering." She nodded to the light. "No strings attached."

"Thanks." He continued to eat. "So what's new?"

"I told the other students you were back today. They all said to say hi and asked when they could see you."

"Tell them hi and I'm sorry for getting their field trips canceled."

She tapped at her tablet. "Are you?"

"Sure. I'm sorry if what I did impacted them." He moved his empty salad plate aside. "I don't regret escaping, and I'll do it again if I get a chance."

"Would you like to apologize in person?" She locked eyes with him. "Maybe you could join them for meals or something."

"That would be nice, but..." He sliced off a piece of rosemary chicken.

"Yes. There is the *but* to deal with. You know my boss wants you tested. Don't get angry with me. We're just talking here. I can't convince him to grant you your privileges back until you agree to some tests."

He dug into the rice pilaf and roast chicken. "What if I took your tests and failed?"

"You won't fail. I know what you're capable of."

"What if I lied?"

She sighed. "We would know."

He nodded with a mouth full of food.

"I understand how you feel, but refusing to cooperate isn't getting us anywhere. Can't we discuss this?"

"Sure. But I don't see any way to compromise."

Stone crossed her legs. "Can I ask you some questions?"

The fork paused partway to his mouth. "You can ask."

"Before you joined us here, you were able to slow down action to give you more time to react to things. This showed up in your athletic endeavors. After you joined us, you improved. Would you say that was because it was easier to slow time? Or because you slowed time even more?"

"That's an interesting distinction." He took his bite.

"Have you—"

He stopped her and swallowed. "I don't think it was easier. I think I got better at it. I think part of it was that for the first time, I had an idea what I was doing."

Stone nodded. "Did skill level diminish during your sabbatical?"

He choked on a mouthful of cranberry juice. "Sabbatical, that's nice." He switched his empty plate for the apple pie. "No vanilla ice cream?"

She uncrossed her legs. "Would you like some?"

"That would be great."

She went to the door and gave the order. When she returned, her smile lit up her face. "It will be here in a moment. Your skills?"

"Hard to say. I didn't have anything to compare it to. I learned to juggle to make cash off the books, so everything about it was different. As I got better at the mechanics, I improved. I only slowed time when I maxed the number I could juggle in order to get more clubs in the air. More clubs equals a bigger crowd. Bigger crowd means more money."

"Are you—" A soft tap at the door interrupted her. She returned with his ice cream. "Are you slowing time now?"

He grinned. "Not at this moment, but I have since I've been back. It passes the time."

"Yes, that would explain why you aren't going stir crazy in here alone all day."

He nodded and dug into his dessert. Her gaze weighed on him. He could hear her synapses firing. When he finished, he pushed the table away. He could almost see the thousands of questions coiled around each other like a pit of vipers inside her head. "What else do you want to know?"

She laughed, and the atmosphere lightened. "So many things. Sadly, you can't answer most of them. Not without my help. Is there anything I can answer for you?"

"I'm wondering where we go from here. I don't think you can answer that without my help."

"You really enjoy using my words against me."

"I don't think of it as using them against you. For me, it reinforces the fact that we are doing our best to be civil. Each of us wants something that is diametrically opposed to the other."

"Wow, diametrically opposed."

Jude held up the book she had given him. "Just learned that one."

"Good night, Jude. Sleep well." Stone left, pushing his dinner cart ahead of her.

In the vacuum of her exit, he considered his recent progress. She wanted to know if the daily injection had helped him manipulate time. She would be shocked at how much progress he'd made in the few days since he'd been back. Before they had caught up to him in California, he'd slowed time enough to earn a living. He had always been present. Someone had needed to catch the clubs, after all. Following the first few injections, things had changed.

The room blurred until it had no detail—no corners, doors, or even furniture, just whiteness sliding toward gray. Then last night he had stepped into what he thought of as an alternate dimension. It had taken him longer to come back from there. It had scared him. *What would happen if I get lost over there? Am I lying here in a coma? Or…or what? Death?* He didn't want to think about that. He needed help, someone to talk with, someone to provide feedback. He had to know what happened to him in his absence.

Do I dream? I know I'm exhausted and hungry. I'm usually soaked in sweat too. Am I walking in my sleep? Or is slipping time enough to deplete my energy? Stone can measure those things. I don't trust her. The nothingness scared him, but he didn't want to admit that, and that bothered him most of all. He didn't know how he could exist in a state of nothingness.

The only person he saw was Stone. Three times a day, she delivered his meals, took his vitals, gave him a shot, and chatted for maybe fifteen minutes. He couldn't share with her. Earlier that evening, their conversation had skipped the mundane and gone straight to the topic. *Maybe I should share my recent exploits with her.* An idea slowly formed in his head. He decided it would be an interesting experiment, one worthy of exposing what he'd been up to to Stone.

The next night, after most everyone had left for the day, he took himself deeper than he'd ever gone before. He walked through darkness as if he were the light source. Setting his fear aside, he experimented. He didn't hear his footsteps. He saw his hands and feet. He waved his arms around, but there was no resistance. He jumped but didn't land exactly. There was no up, no down, and no gravity.

When he came to, he had no recollection of time passing. Sleep had kidnapped him.

Dr. Stone shook him awake. But he was out of it, as if he'd been drugged.

"Jude, are you feeling okay?"

"Huh, tired. So tired." He tried to roll over, but Stone held his shoulder.

"Jude, what did you do last night? What's going on? You're soaked."

The concern in her voice reached him, and he tried to shake himself awake. His clothes stuck to him. He ran a hand over his sweat-slicked face. "Sorry, Doctor. I-I need a shower. Can you give me a few minutes?"

"I'll leave your breakfast and come back."

When she left, he pushed himself up and got into the shower. He had to climb out of this funk, or she would have ten doctors poking him in places no one should be poked.

Baird was sipping his tea when a tap on the door precluded Stone walking in. She took a seat across from him.

"Dr. Stone, what brings you to my office?"

"Look, Baird, I know we have our differences, but I'm worried about Jude." She passed him her tablet.

Baird watched the video of her trying to wake Jude. "This is a little disconcerting. May I ask if you've tinkered with the formula of his injection?"

"I'm having that double-checked, but to answer your question, no, we haven't changed it. Unless someone made a mistake."

Baird hoped for the sake of the chemist that it wasn't a mistake. Stone would have them escorted out of the building before lunch if it was. "What else is going on with him?"

"I don't know. I'm going to have a medical team work him up today after his breakfast. I want you to look over all their data. If it's not physical…"

"Of course I'll review all the data and confer with the medical team on their findings. I'll review the video record from his room. Maybe he's training for a marathon at night."

"This is no joke, Doctor."

"No, of course it's not. I'm serious. It would not be beneath him to exert himself overnight to skew your tests."

"The overnight crew is supposed to report any unusual activity. If he were doing laps around his bed all night, they would have noticed. Don't you think?"

"I don't know what they do all night. It must get a little boring." Baird knew that the overnight team spent most of their time in the game room, holding tournaments. Like so many things that went on around the compound, the less Stone knew, the better for everyone.

She stood up. "You'll let me know what you find?"

"I'll reach you as soon as I see anything unusual."

It was the first time in months Stone left his office without slamming the door. *She must be worried.* Baird pulled up the current feed from Jude's room. He practically inhaled his breakfast. Other than that, Baird didn't see anything strange. He logged in the time and date of Jude's arrival back at the facility and fast-forwarded through the first interaction with Dr. Stone. From that point, he played the tape two times normal speed.

He saw that odd flicker again and stopped the feed then replayed it in real time. Jude seemed to fade from the screen for a brief moment. *Is it a trick of the lighting?* He didn't think so. He noted the time and moved on. He'd been watching every minute of Jude's captivity for hours. *I need a break.* He stopped the playback and went down to the dining hall.

After Jude's breakfast, four doctors came in and started running tests on him. They started with the usual blood work and vitals. He then agreed to a full body scan and a stress test. He was exhausted, and the stress test taxed him. He decided to cooperate with them. He didn't have the energy to fight them. But more to the point, he wanted Dr. Stone relaxed when she came to see him that night. He didn't know if what he'd planned was even possible. But he decided to try it out that night or maybe the next morning, depending on how he felt.

No sooner had the doctors left him alone in his room than Stone came in through the door with his lunch. She had been hovering during most of the tests, but they hadn't talked at all.

She pushed the cart over to his bed and took the chair next to him. "How are you feeling?"

"I'm tired. I read last night but not that long."

"Thanks for your cooperation today. I know that went against your grain."

"I didn't want to make you look bad in front of the other doctors." He uncovered his lunch. "Do I have the flu or something?"

"Not as far as we can tell. They said you're suffering from mild malnutrition. You aren't throwing up your meals, are you, Jude?"

He laughed. "Not hardly. I'm starving." He took a moment to chew and swallow a bite. Then he motioned to his plate, which contained a large serving of grilled fish and broccoli. "It looks like the chef got the memo on my appetite."

"The doctors said you are run-down, sleep-deprived, and on the verge of anemia. Have you had any breaks with reality?"

"How would I know if I did? My reality isn't real. I've been isolated in solitary confinement. Even today, those guys didn't talk to me as much as point and grunt." He imitated their flat, toneless directions. "Sit here, take a breath, lie down, stand up."

"Yes. I'm sorry, but I was worried about you. I told them to find out what's going on with you as quickly as possible. I'm afraid I didn't use those exact words."

Jude nodded with a mouthful of food.

She put a hand on his arm. "Jude, can we be honest here?"

"We have been honest, haven't we, Doctor?"

"I think we have. I think you know what's going on with you. Would you tell me if you did?"

"I might know. But I'm not ready to share just yet. Maybe after dinner. Let me think about it."

She sighed. "That's honest."

He had vanquished his lunch and pushed the tray away. "I think I'll take a nap."

After a quick check of his vitals, she left. He crashed immediately.

Baird returned to reviewing Jude's activity. The health reports were trickling in. There was some concern about his general lack of energy and a question about nutrition, but nothing startling. His health looked like that of a young man working two jobs while eating from a vending machine and maintaining a social life. The problem was that Jude spent his day confined to a 144-square-foot room and ate three meals a day. So where did his resources get used up? The doctors were searching for an immune deficiency, but they were coming up empty.

Baird emailed a preliminary report to Stone that pretty much said they needed to wait and see. It left with a whoosh. *She'll love that.* He settled in and started the playback again. His eyes watered from so many hours of watching the screen. By and large, Jude never moved. He used the bathroom, showered, and ate. He spent the rest of his time sleeping or reading.

Nothing added up. Jude had been in better health when he was living in a van. Baird decided to stay late to get through the video, knowing full well that Stone would be on the warpath the next day if Jude continued to decline.

Baird shook his head, disbelieving what he'd just seen. He

backed the time stamp on the video feed and played it again at real time, then again at half speed. He called IT to see if they could explain the anomaly. He reviewed the video over and over. Each time, Jude faded from the screen. IT called back. They were looking into it, but they had no answers. Baird finally moved on to see when and how Jude would reappear. Two hours and thirty-seven seconds later, Jude reappeared. He thrashed on the bed for a minute before falling fast asleep. He looked as if he'd been running. His breathing was rapid, and his skin glistened as though he were coated in sweat.

Baird fired off an email to Stone, asking her to come to his office right away. He'd been at this all night, and his mind was a little fuzzy. When he realized morning had arrived and she was in the building, he paged her. She didn't respond. He viewed Jude's return several more times. Then he switched to the current feed from Jude's room. Stone was sitting in the chair next to him.

Baird hurried from his office down to the observation room. Fear coated his throat. He paged Stone several more times as he walked. At Jude's room, he tried his security badge. A flashing red light informed him he did not have approval to access the door. He knocked.

The door opened. "What is it, Doctor? I'm busy."

"There's something you should see. I've been watching the playback from Jude's room, and well, you should see it for yourself."

She rolled her eyes. "Did you sleep in your clothes last night?"

"I didn't sleep. I watched Jude's video all night. You really need to see this."

"Fine. I'll be out shortly."

"You don't understand. It's not—"

The door closed in his face. He went back to the observation room and sat down in front of the mirror.

Jude pushed his empty plate away. He'd only heard a little of the conversation at the door. But the urgency Baird had used made him think it was now or never. He didn't slip time last night so he was well-rested.

Dr. Stone moved the cart away from the bed. "So where were we?"

"You were asking if I'd given our conversation at lunch any thought."

"And have you?"

He sat up straight and concentrated. Maintaining his concentration was critical. He wasn't sure about how to do this. But intuitively, he knew his concentration would have to be absolute. He listened to his rhythmic breathing and the regular thump of his heart. He slowed his breathing. "Yes, I have." His voice sounded dreamy. He closed his eyes.

"Jude, are you feeling all right? You seem a little out of it."

"Yes, I feel fine. Thank you for asking. How about yourself, Doctor?"

"You're acting a little strangely."

"I'm feeling a little out of it."

"What's going on, Jude?"

"You'll be pleased to hear I have radically changed my position on cooperating with your research." He opened his eyes and tried for his most charming smile. "I would like you to see what your treatments have done for me."

Dr. Stone gave him a wary look. "I must say I'm surprised."

"I've had, what, three, four days to reconsider." Jude tilted his head. "It would seem we are at a stalemate. You know, the thing they talk about in physics? The immovable object meets the irresistible force. Something had to give."

"And which am I?"

"Dr. Stone, you shouldn't have to ask. You're clearly an irresistible force."

She stood, concern coloring her features. "Do you mind if I check your vitals?"

"Not at all. You're the doctor, Doctor." He patted the edge of the bed. "Come, have a listen to my change of heart."

Dr. Stone checked his pulse first and frowned slightly. "It's a little slow."

Jude closed his eyes and slipped a little deeper. Time slowed, and he no longer felt the bed pressing against his rear.

Dr. Stone pulled a blood pressure cuff from one pocket of her lab coat and a stethoscope from the other. "Have you felt dizzy?" She applied the cuff and pumped it up.

Jude placed one hand lightly on her elbow and went deeper. Light faded to gray, and he floated on the first wave of timelessness.

"Jude?"

"Hmmm?"

"What's happening?" She tried to pull away from him, but he tightened his grip.

Baird watched the exchange like someone at the scene of a gruesome accident. Something was wrong, but he couldn't tear his gaze from the scene before him. Panic blossomed on Stone's face, and she struggled to pull free of Jude's grip. Baird picked up the receiver and punched in twelve twelve.

"Security," the voice drawled.

"I think Dr. Stone's in trouble. She's in observation room two hundred."

"I'll send someone down."

"You'd better hurry."

Baird couldn't believe what he was seeing. He dropped the receiver to the floor. "It may be too late," he said to no one as Stone and Jude faded from the screen. One moment, they were there. In the next, he saw through them as they became less substantial. Then they were gone. Baird wondered if they were coming back, or if like Elvis, they had left the building for good.

Sunset On Shaman Butte

J oe guided his four-wheel-drive Chevy pickup over the rough desert terrain. The recent rains in the mountains nearby had turned the area into a moonscape. The Arizona desert was laced with interwoven dry washes, over which water coursed during the rainy season. The pattern of lace changed every season from the unrelenting force of water cascading to the desert floor from the surrounding mountains. Joe knew his way through the maze of washes, but he wished he had given himself more time.

"How much farther is it?" Debbie asked.

He stole a glance at Debbie's bust. "We're almost there. Wait until you see the sunsets out here. Then you'll understand why I love this place."

This relationship business presented new challenges for Joe. Cutting yearlings out of the herd was easier than a new relationship. He hoped Debbie would not be disappointed.

"Do you remember the day we met?" she asked.

"Sure." He smiled. "You were covered in hay when

that bale busted open."

"I have a confession to make."

Joe eased up on the accelerator. "What's that?"

"I cut the twine."

"On purpose?"

"I flirted with you for weeks, and you wouldn't look at me. I had to do something."

"You wasted a bale of hay so I would ask you out."

"I paid Old Man Peters for the bale, and I asked *you* out if you remember."

"Yeah. How could I forget? A picnic lunch, fried chicken, tater salad, and cold beer."

"And homemade apple pie, don't forget."

Joe pushed the accelerator, sensing it was getting late.

Debbie rubbed his arm gently. "What are you smiling about?"

"Nothing. Just thinking. Woolgathering, that's what Pa calls it." He pointed toward the horizon, where the sun was dropping out of the sky. The truck bounced in and out of a rut that had gotten past Joe's radar.

Debbie squeaked in surprise. "Why is it that no one ever comes out here? Besides you, I mean."

"There's an Indian legend about this area. I don't put much stock in those old ghost stories."

"Let's hear it."

"I'll tell it after we get there." Joe needed to be on time for the sunset. He knew instinctively by the way the afternoon broke with an occasional high cloud that the sunset over Shaman Butte would be a kaleidoscope of blues and pinks. The gentle breeze drifting over the desert surface would keep them comfortable. And if they were lucky, the colors would mutate to vibrant oranges and purples as the sun completed its westward journey.

The terrain grew rougher, and Joe concentrated on

keeping the shiny side of his truck skyward as he raced the sun to its destiny with the horizon. Another large rut jarred Debbie across the seat, and she landed right next to him.

He forced a smile. "It's worth the trip. You wait and see."

She put her hand on his knee and held on. Joe focused his full attention on navigating. He spun the wheel sharply left then right, downshifting to allow the truck to coast down the side of a shallow ravine. Then he accelerated. The tires spun as the truck clawed up the other side of the embankment. Sand and gravel yielded as the truck responded to his commands.

Happiness and dread washed over him in alternating waves. He felt happy the truck he had wanted for so long was living up to his expectations, and dread because Debbie's fingers were digging into his leg so hard that he thought blood must have been oozing down his calf. At the very least, his new boot-cut Wranglers would have five crescent-shaped holes in the fabric. From the bottom of a narrow wash, he lost sight of the sun for a moment.

Afraid the sun might decide to set without them, he pushed the truck for more speed. He downshifted and gunned the engine in one fluid move. The truck climbed. Nothing but sky could be seen through the windshield. Debbie's grip tightened on Joe's leg. At the top of the wash, Shaman Butte came into view. Lit by the retreating sun, it glowed as if the rock emitted its own light.

Debbie inhaled sharply when Joe stopped the truck at the top of the ridge. "It's beautiful," she whispered.

He recognized the tree line. They'd made it. "My spot's just over there." He nodded his head. His cowboy hat sat slightly askew, but it guided Debbie's gaze toward a pretty oasis. Joe parked at the ideal place to watch Mother Nature paint another masterpiece.

Hundreds of butterflies hovered around the sage bushes and mesquite trees. Again, Debbie's sharp inhale accompanied an adoring gaze at the natural beauty.

Joe helped Debbie into the back of the truck, and they sat on an old quilt. From a cooler, he produced cold bottles of water and a single pink rose. She opened her mouth, but Joe gently put his finger to her lips and nodded toward Shaman Butte. Debbie watched as the sun sat atop the butte as if it were resting. A short time later, as it dropped from sight, it painted the bottoms of the clouds cotton-candy pastels. Fifteen minutes later, the colors changed to bruised blues and deep oranges.

For the first time in an hour, Joe allowed himself to relax. They watched silently while nature provided the entertainment.

"Didn't I tell y—"

This time, Debbie placed a finger over Joe's lips. She leaned over and gently brushed his lips with her own. His insides turned to jelly, and Debbie whispered, "I get it."

Again, she leaned in and pressed her lips to his. Joe's heart soared. They had kissed before, but this was the first time she'd initiated it. As the sun crossed the horizon, Joe realized that life didn't get any better. His new truck had delivered him and his girlfriend to his favorite place on earth.

When he looked into Debbie's eyes, a sensation of vertigo swept over him. He sensed a special connection, one that didn't require talking.

Dusk ushered in an unearthly stillness. The afternoon breezes bedded down, and the nocturnal wildlife had yet to emerge. A lone hummingbird hovered over an ocotillo bush.

Debbie broke the silence. "You were going to tell me why no one comes out here."

"Are you sure you want to hear this now? I mean, here."

"I'm not afraid of an old ghost story."

"Okay. Well, these Apache braves were hunting near here. The tribe had been kept on the run by a troop of Union soldiers, and they were near starving. A powerful medicine man rode with them to bring them success. They stumbled into the cavalry by accident. It was the same troop that had been chasing their people. The hunting party decided to lead them away from the rest of the tribe. So they rode into this area, hoping to lose the soldiers in these dry washes.

"The army used Ute trackers, making it hard for the Apaches to lose them. They traveled around here for days, doubling back, moving at night, and erasing their trail. Every night, they would widen the gap, and each day, the soldiers would close it. After trying all the tricks they knew, hungry and tired, they turned to the medicine man.

"They would have to risk getting caught to give the shaman time to pray. They built a small shelter for him. He sat for two days with nothing to eat or drink, sweating over a small fire, praying to First Woman. When he finally emerged, he led them to this streambed." Joe motioned toward the tree line. "They knew the soldiers were close by. The shaman told them the army would be there in the morning, riding from the south. The hunting party had to wait on the north bank of the streambed until he gave them a signal. Then they were to ride hard, whooping it up to attract the soldiers' attention. The medicine man chanted and danced all that night at the stream. Right after dawn, the braves saw a dust cloud approaching. They mounted and waited for the signal. They also prepared to die. The hooves of the cavalry horses thundered toward their position. The shaman finally gave the signal, and the hunting party rode hell-bent for leather. When they looked back, they saw no sign of the soldiers or their shaman. They carefully backtracked on foot to the streambed, certain it was a trap. At the stream, they saw the tracks of the horses riding in, but none riding out. The only sign the soldiers had been there at all was a hat belonging to one of the Union soldiers, sitting in the middle of the streambed."

"So the cavalry disappeared, horses and all?" Debbie asked.

"That's the story."

"And that's this streambed we're parked next to now?"

"Yep." Joe pointed. "The medicine man danced right where you see that big, gnarled-up mesquite tree."

"What about the medicine man?"

"Never turned up."

"Joe Washburn, that's ridiculous."

"I can't vouch for that story, but one time, I saw a brand-new quad sitting in that same streambed up to its axles in muck. The engine ticked, the way it will when it's still hot. I yelled for the driver, but no one answered. The quad slipped deeper into the mud. I was going to try to pull it out, but by the time I moved my truck close enough, the roll bar and windshield were all I could see. I couldn't believe it. I watched it get pulled down until it disappeared. A large air bubble gurgled up, leaving no sign anything had been there at all except for a Diamondbacks cap. That's when I looked for footprints. There weren't any."

"Now you're trying to scare me."

"True story. I swear."

"I may have been born at night, but I wasn't born last night."

"I'm telling you true. Lots of people go missing in this part of the desert."

"Joseph Washburn, I'm telling your mother."

"Just forget it." Joe pulled away. "I'm no liar."

"I'm sorry." Debbie snuggled up against him. "Don't get mad."

He stiffened.

She surprised him with a passionate kiss but suddenly broke it off. "Do you hear that?"

"I don't hear anyth—" In the distance, Joe detected engine noise. Then banging and rattling reached his ears.

"You hear it now?"

"What in tarnation is that?" He stood up on the side rail and looked across the desert in the fading light of evening.

"It's probably one of those people who disappear out here." She patted the quilt. "Sit down."

"Hold on. I see something."

Out of the dust emerged a familiar shape—a dark-brown delivery truck. "I don't believe it."

Debbie joined him, balancing on the rail. "Where do you think he's going?"

"He's going down to unemployment when the company finds out what he's done to that truck."

"No, really, where is he going?"

"I don't know. There's nothing but hundreds of square miles of empty desert out there."

"There must be something out there. Those guys have computers and GPS units. They don't just go driving around in the desert for no apparent reason."

"I'm telling you!" Joe's temper flared. "There is nothing out there."

She persisted. "Maybe it's a secret government facility, and Joe Washburn was not on the need-to-know list."

"Right. A secret government facility, and Dougie's driving in from Queens with a package. Do you think it's next-day or regular ground?"

"You don't have to be a smart-ass about it. I just think he must know where he's going."

"Sorry, but there is no way he knows where he's going unless he came out here to wreck that truck." Joe watched as the truck approached the ancient mesquite tree. "I think he's going to try to cross the creek bed. He'll never make it in that boat."

The truck easily navigated its way into the stream, passed the tree, and drove up the other side.

"Isn't that where you claim you saw a whole quad disappear?" Debbie's tone mocked him.

Joe jumped to the ground. "I can't believe it."

"Where're you going?"

"After that truck. Let's just see if he knows where he's going."

Debbie stared at him. "Are you kidding?"

"What's the matter? You scared?"

Debbie jumped down and climbed into the truck, shrugging off his help. "Let's go, or maybe you're afraid we'll disappear." She pulled her hair into a ponytail.

Joe slammed the door and drove straight toward the old tree. He would show her. But when he approached the creek bed, his stomach became a hornet's nest. Without conscious thought, he slammed on the brakes and cut a hard left, throwing Debbie against the passenger door. A glance told him it was too little, too late.

He slipped into reverse and eased his booted foot off the clutch. The tires spun slowly, but the truck didn't move. He opened the door of the truck and looked down then shifted into first and tried to move forward. Finally, he floored the accelerator. The tires whined. Muck thudded against the undercarriage and flew into the air. Joe pounded the steering wheel and leapt out. Getting his bearings, he backed away from the truck a few more steps.

"Get out of the truck," Joe whispered. He didn't want the mud to hear the fear in his voice.

Debbie opened the passenger door.

"No!" He looked around and whispered, "Slide to this side of the truck. When I say go, you jump like you're going to kick me in the chest."

Debbie rolled her eyes and started out her door but suddenly froze. When she turned back to Joe, the color had drained from her face. Her bottom lip quivered, and tears shone in her eyes.

"Come on, Debbie, you can do this. Slide over to this side and jump out."

She looked at Joe, and a moan escaped her lips.

"Damn it. Come on before it's too late! Jump. I'll catch you. I promise." Joe watched his new truck slip deeper. Blood pounded in his ears as he watched two years of hard work disappear. "Damn it, Debbie, get over here!"

Debbie quieted and brushed the last tear from her face. The truck gave up resisting and started sinking faster. Primordial ooze coated the floor. She pulled her feet onto the seat, kneeling behind the steering wheel. "I'm sorry, Joe. I should have believed you."

"How about that?" Joe planted his hands on his hips. "Now let's go. We've got a long walk ahead of us."

In a whisper, she said, "We're not going anywhere." She pointed a trembling finger at Joe's feet.

He watched her ashen face assume a calm demeanor. "What are you talking about?"

She nodded, lowering her gaze.

Comprehension dawned when he saw his silver-and-turquoise belt buckle disappear below the surface of the mud.

Dawn broke over the dry streambed in the shadow of Shaman Butte. A sweat-stained cowboy hat rested in its midst.

Life's A Carnival

W ill's cash reserves were thinning faster than the
     crowd on the midway. Barkers called half-heart-
edly from their games. Vicky clutched an immense stuffed
panda he'd won from popping balloons with darts. It had
cost him a small fortune. He was good at darts, a relatively
easy skill he'd honed in his father's basement. But his
swagger and confidence were the very things the crooked
men who ran these games counted on. They relied on guys
like Will for their livelihood. They had tricks he would
never learn. He steered Vicky between the Wheel of
Fortune and the Shooting Gallery toward the rides.

Screams battled for room in the night air, while
"Layla" leaped from the tortured speakers at the Bobsled.
Scents of fried food and cotton candy filled the summer
air, clinging to his skin. Past the Tilt-a-Whirl, a fat man sat
on a stool near the entrance to the Tunnel of Love. He
leered and winked as he took Will's money.

Vicky's look of dread hit him square on. "I don't
like rides."

"This is tame, no spinning or sudden movements." Will

heard the pleading in his voice and hated it. "It's just a boat ride in the dark. Don't be a fraidy-cat."

"I'm not scared. It's just... They're kinda creepy." Vicky nodded toward the fat man and the attendant, who steadied their boat, and grimaced at the greasy wifebeater he wore. When she stepped up, he smiled, showing a few crooked, tobacco-stained teeth.

Will stepped between her and the carny with a false show of bravado. He took the panda and helped Vicky sit. Once he was settled next to her, he nodded.

"Enjoy the ride." With a sinister laugh, the carny pushed off the boat.

The temperature dropped when they bumped through the heart-shaped tunnel entrance. Will pulled Vicky close. Water dripped from the dark. The heavy air smelled stagnant. Ominous music played from everywhere at once. The tune was either on a short loop or stuck—he wasn't sure which—but the repetitive melody caused his muscles to tense.

"Something's off," Vicky whispered. "Can you smell that?"

He sniffed. An odor had gathered under the dampness. *Roadkill.* Something had died in there. His guess was a rat, which wasn't something he would share with Vicky. She was freaking already. "Yeah. It's that guy's body odor."

She pulled away from him.

"Relax. We'll be out soon."

The weird music got louder, the stench intensified, and the boat bumped along in the unending darkness.

"I'm cold."

He pulled her close. She *was* cold. Too cold. "Better?"

She didn't reply.

The ride should have been over by then. He assured himself that what seemed like hours had only been minutes. He reached out to ensure they were moving. The wall recoiled at his touch as if it were alive. He swallowed back vomit and jerked his hand away. *What the hell was that?* "Sorry. I got a cramp."

Vicky still didn't respond.

"Vicky? You okay?"

She said nothing. He gently shook her. "Vicky?" He turned and grabbed her shoulders. "Vicky!"

She slumped forward. Cold, she was so cold. He lifted her chin as if to kiss her, and her desiccated flesh slid through his fingers. The stench of death filled his nostrils. He retched the contents of his stomach. The odor mixed with the smell of her decomposing body. Impulsively, he stood to jump from the boat, but the memory of the wall flinching away from his touch held him fast. He realized in that moment that Vicky was the lucky one. She had escaped. His scream lifted from his throat like a rocket searing through the atmosphere.

The boat bumped along the infinite tunnel. The eternal music played. Will's scream joined the legion.

Restoration of Sanity

A corns crunched beneath the tires of George Shaw's truck as he drove into the circular driveway guarded by ancient oak trees. The musty air smelled of abandonment and rotting vegetation. The odors combined with the sting of the chilly autumn morning, cloaking him in a dark shroud of depression. *Autumn colors, my ass. Fall is the Harbinger of Death. Winter will be here any day.*

For the first time since he'd started his business, he didn't have enough work on the books to keep his crew busy through the thin months. He'd gotten his hopes up when he received the invitation to look at this job, until he'd heard the Historical Society was involved. *The fastest way to stop a job before it started is to involve the Hysterical Society. I'll end up wasting a day or more putting numbers together for a job that will never happen.*

At the end of the polished black hood of his F-250 stood a neglected 150-year-old plantation-style home, faded to the same lifeless shade of gray as the November sky. On the expansive porch, in spiked heels, stood his appointment.

He parked next to her Lexus then grabbed a tape measure and clipboard off the passenger seat. *This day won't be a total loss.*

Long legs led the way to a shapely rear. At his approach, the woman spun on her heel. The gray wool business suit had red pinstripes and a tight skirt with a strategically placed slit at the back. The skirt hit just below her knee. George got a tasty glimpse of her thighs before she turned around. A conservative red silk blouse and shoulder-length raven-black hair as shiny as George's truck completed the look.

"You must be George." She extended her right hand and flashed a smile that completely undermined his foundation. The toe of his boot caught on the first step, which sent him sprawling. His chin landed inches from her shapely ankles. Heat radiated off his neck and face. When he tilted his head up to apologize, he found himself looking up her skirt.

Hastily, he turned away, not that he'd seen much. But the feeling of impropriety held his voice captive in his throat. "S-s-s-sorry. I'm not usually clumsy." In his peripheral vision, he caught sight of her hand offering to help him up. "Just have the demolition crew haul me away when they get here."

Her light laugh floated above him. "Don't be silly. I'm sure that's not the first time you've fallen. I'd be willing to bet you've experienced far worse in your line of work."

He dusted himself off. "Somehow, it's not as embarrassing in front of a bunch of beer-drinking, loud-mouthed wood butchers who depend on me for their checks."

"I'm Shari O'Brien. I'm coordinating the project for the Bucks County Historical Society."

"George Shaw, Blue Moon Restoration, contractor and klutz. Nice to meet you."

"Let me show you around a little."

"Lead the way, and I promise to stay on my feet." He followed her inside. "I did a little research on the property after your call. It has quite a story to tell. I hope you don't mind my jumping ahead, but if I can cut to the chase here, I might save us both a lot of time."

Shari stopped just inside the entrance hall and looked back. Framed in the massive space, she appeared fragile. "By all means."

"It's been my experience that groups such as the Historical Society mean well but rarely have the resources to restore a property this large the way it should be done." He tried to bite back his next thought, but his jaws kept flapping. "That is to say, the way my firm would do it. So do you have a budget number in mind?" He needed this job, but he would not do it half-assed.

Shari straightened and gave him a hard look. "I have to say, you *do* get right to the point. I didn't call you out here to waste your time, Mr. Shaw. I too have done my homework. We've already decided to offer you a position as a consultant until we can develop a scope of work. You would be paid to do the research you've already started. The plan is to establish the property's place in Bucks County's history. I actually represent a group of businessmen who are interested in restoring this property.

"We"—she gestured to George and herself—"will work closely with the Historical Society. When the project is complete, they will become the custodians of the property. So you see, money isn't really the issue. Now, would you like to see the property, or do you want to refer me to someone else?"

"I didn't mean to offend. It's just—"

"Fine." She spun on her heel and continued into the

house. "Now that we've gotten the crudities out of the way, let's have a look at what we're up against."

George tried to recover his equilibrium. "As I mentioned, this grand lady has a great story to tell."

"Then you probably know the home was built around 1850 by Dr. Hood. He also owned the surrounding three thousand acres, on which he raised cattle and horses."

"Yes. But it was more of a gentleman's farm." George relaxed a little. "Dr. Hood treated the locals for their ailments. In return, he received labor and produce as payment. His passion for horses cost him more money than he made. He raised everything from Clydesdales to Arabians. The real story is about Gretchen Hood, his young wife, who abhorred slavery. She convinced her husband to take part in the Underground Railroad, providing a hideaway, food, and medical treatment to slaves fleeing the South. Many of them stayed on to work for the Hoods as free people. Mrs. Hood and her work as an abolitionist serve as the human-interest side of the story, giving the property historical significance beyond the date it was built." George took a breath and stepped into the library. "Aside from that, the doctor installed some unique architectural features into the home, such as a shaft from the icehouse to the main house. He utilized convection air currents to create the first air-conditioned home."

Shari gaped at him. "You learned all that in just one day? I'm quite impressed. I see I've made the right decision selecting you to spearhead this project."

George paused to look up at the intricate plaster work around the ceiling. "May I ask how you heard about Blue Moon Restoration?"

"One of the men I represent suggested I look into your company. Your references praise your results." Shari hesitated before continuing. "Some say you can be... difficult to work with."

"Difficult?" *I've got nothing on the Hysterical Society.* "I can be a downright pain in the ass sometimes, always in the interest of maintaining historical accuracy. Who did you say recommended me?"

Mild amusement danced across Shari's face. "Do you know the law firm Johnson, Johnson, and Johnson?"

He chuckled, suppressing his distaste for lawyers. "Can't say I do."

"That's no matter. Did your research turn up anything... strange?"

"What do you mean by strange?"

"You know—things out of the ordinary, such as ghosts or unusual occurrences."

George laughed. "I'm sorry. I don't mean to be rude, but I specialize in restoring historical properties. I haven't worked on one yet that doesn't have a ghost story. Most of them are just legends created before our entertainment was spoon-fed to us via Hollywood or the Internet."

Shari looked relieved. "That's good to know."

"The only spirits my crew have ever encountered are the kind that come from a bottle." He laughed, but Shari did not join him. "My research focuses on architecture, styles of craftsmanship, and building materials available at the time the house was built. Once the home was abandoned by the Hood children, I stopped looking."

Shari's phone buzzed softly in her purse. She pulled it out and glanced at it. "That's the boss man now." She held her phone up. "I've got to take this."

"I'll have a look around." His footsteps echoed in the empty, spacious rooms. Hand-planed moldings, vaulted plaster ceilings, and inlaid hardwood floors confronted him at every turn. He marveled at the condition of the twelve-foot-high double-hung windows designed to circulate air to cool the house in the temperate months. It was unusual to find a home this old that hadn't been chopped up into offices, apartments, or worst of all, vandalized. In truth, some builders achieved far worse damage under the guise of remodeling than any group of irresponsible teens.

Outside, he inspected the wraparound porch, structurally sound but in dire need of cosmetic work to restore it back to its former glory as the pre-entrance of the home. He felt the weight of the second-story windows staring down on him through their multicolored panes as he passed through what must have been beautiful gardens in their day. He imagined the voices of the work crew as they labored and could almost smell the freshly sawn lumber.

He hesitated at the stone steps that led to a cellar. Shari's voice echoed through the empty rooms. She was evidently still on the phone. The flashlight on his phone was insufficient to properly inspect the basement, but he decided to have a look-see. Major structural problems would be easy to identify in any light. Futilely, he waved one arm through the air to keep the cobwebs off his face. The dark strengthened the farther he ventured from the entrance. The walls were coated with a crystalline substance, probably a reaction of the lime in the cement used to hold the stones in place.

The emptiness of the basement felt endless. He should have found the front wall by then. The cellar shouldn't have been larger than the house. He made a mental note to measure it later. A shuffling noise left him holding his breath. He listened but only heard deafening quiet. "Hello, is someone down here?"

Murmuring voices floated on the air. Slowly, he turned around, trying to pinpoint what direction they'd come from. "Ms. O'Brien?" He didn't like the shrill sound of his own voice. Something scrabbled across the dirt floor. He spun, searching for a rat. The air grew warm and carried the strong scent of unwashed bodies. The pungent smell overwhelmed him. Someone was living down there, probably squatters. He scanned the area with his useless phone, the light reaching only a few feet in front of him. "Come out where I can see you. I mean you no harm." They would be evicted, but thankfully, that was not his job. Sweat formed on his face and ran into his eyes.

The murmuring returned, louder than before.

"I'm calling the police if you don't show yourself."

A metallic rattle accompanied a flickering orange glow. George closed his eyes for a moment to improve his night vision. The flickering grew brighter until George made out the whites of a pair of eyes. Straining to see, he made out a black man clothed in tatters. The man held a dangerous-looking sickle in one hand and a lantern in the other.

"What are you doing down here?" George asked.

"The missus sent us. My Ruby be needin' some doctorin'."

A vague gesture led George's gaze to the silhouette of a woman on the floor. He directed his feeble light at her. She lay in a pile of dirty straw, her belly swollen. In her mouth, a stick was nearly bitten in two. Tears streamed down her face.

"It's our first. My Ruby's a-scared."

"We need to get you to a hospital." George reached a hand down to help the woman up. "Give me a hand there."

The man's eyes grew larger, and the hand holding the sickle twitched.

George backed away one step and held up his hands. "Hold on there. I'm not going to hurt her."

"Can you help my Ruby?"

George lifted his phone to call 911. "I'll call somebody."

Ruby let out a muffled scream that raised the hair on the back of George's neck. He blinked at his phone. *No service.* "Well, that just figures, doesn't it?" He'd seen a video of an emergency delivery in a first-aid class he'd taken a few years ago, but he never expected he would be in a position to need it. His use of first aid was limited to on the job, where he mostly stemmed the flow of blood until the professionals arrived.

Ruby lifted her head off the ground and screamed again.

"You help my Ruby." The man nodded toward the young woman in distress, and again, the sickle hand twitched.

George pulled off his new company jacket and laid it between the woman's legs. "Let's have a look at what we're dealing with, shall we?" The crown of the baby's head was visible in the light of his phone. "Oh shit, oh shit, oh shit! Okay, Ruby, I know it hurts." He took the stick from between her teeth. "Pant, you know, like a dog." He demonstrated then looked up at the man. "We need water and some clean towels."

The man looked down at him, stupefied.

"Go get some help. Tell Ms. O'Brien to call 911."

"Pant, Ruby. Pant." Again, he demonstrated. He tried to remember what he'd learned. "You scream all you want." He adjusted his jacket. "It's almost here, Ruby. Breathe." He looked up, astonished to see the man watching him. "What are you still doing here? Go! Now!" He pointed with one hand, indicating the direction the man should go.

"I can't leave my Ruby."

Ruby grunted and lifted her upper body off the floor.

Her face turned a dark shade of red, and her features scrunched up.

"I'm not ready for this!" George glanced down. The baby's head poked out, covered in silky black hair. He bit his tongue until it bled to keep from passing out. Resigning himself to the task at hand, he crouched low and extended a hand to support the baby. "Keep pushing. Good girl. It's almost here."

Sweat burned George's eyes in spite of the cool air. After the head popped out, the baby slid into his waiting hands. "It's a boy," he yelled in his excitement. The only thing keeping him from losing it was the adrenaline raging through his veins. He wrapped the baby in his jacket and passed him to the mother. "I just delivered a baby! Damn. Double goddamn! What's his name?"

"Jeremiah. Jeremiah Johnson." They were the first words he heard her speak. She moved Jeremiah to her waiting breast and sighed.

"Wait here," George said. "I'm going to get you some help." He ran through the basement, keeping his head down and watching his phone for the first sign of a signal. He didn't stop until he topped the steps. He panted when the operator picked up. "I just delivered a baby at…" He couldn't remember the street address. "It's the old Hood plantation house on Township Line Road." The operator rattled off an address. "Yeah, that's the place."

"George. Shaw." Shari clipped each word.

He turned to see her looking none too pleased. Ignoring her, he continued talking to the 911 operator. "The mother's name is Ruby Johnson. I think they're homeless."

"Mr. Shaw! I've been looking all over for you. Where the hell did you disappear to?" Stepping down from the back door, Shari looked as if he'd pissed in her Wheaties.

"A man, maybe thirtyish. The mother's young. And the baby. Damn right, I'm staying on the line until they arrive." He heard the dead air of hold and turned his attention to Shari. She was charging across the yard, not an easy task in those shoes.

He waved and smiled. "Hey, I was in the basement, and the most amazing—"

"You were in the basement all this time? You must be kidding me."

"No. I just delivered a baby to a woman down there. I think they may be living there."

Shari stopped right in front of him, her nostrils flaring. "You what?"

"I delivered a baby."

"Down there?" She motioned with her hand. "Why didn't you pick up my call?"

He shrugged. "No signal."

She started down the steps. "Are you coming?"

"I'm going out to the road to wave the ambulance in." He heard a small voice and realized he'd forgotten the 911 call. "I'm still here, Operator." He started toward the road, waving to Shari as she descended the steps.

Out by the street, he thought about what had just happened. *Where did they come from with that deep southern drawl? And who did he say sent them down there?* He hunched his shoulders. *What a morning!* He saw the flashing lights of an approaching patrol car. He disconnected the call and put his phone away. Desperately, he tried to regain his equilibrium. A November wind rattled what leaves remained on the trees. He shivered as a chill stalked up his back.

"Did you call in a medical emergency?" the officer asked for the second time, jerking him out of his spinning thoughts.

"Yes. There are two people in the cellar. I think they may be living there. The woman had a baby."

The cop started pulling away. "Wait here for the ambulance."

"Around the back of the house," George yelled after the departing patrol car.

The ambulance barely slowed before turning into the driveway. George jogged after them. When he rounded the house, he saw the officer, two EMTs, and Shari all in conversation. Why weren't they bringing out Ruby and Jeremiah?

"What are you waiting for?" he asked as he reached the huddle.

"Are you Mr. Shaw?" the cop asked.

"Of course," he snapped.

"Can I see some ID?"

"Yeah, but someone needs to go down and check on the baby first." He handed over his driver's license and spun to face the paramedic. "Go get them, for Christ's sake."

"Relax, Mr. Shaw." The officer took him by the elbow, and one of the paramedics took him by the other one. "Everything is under control."

They guided him to the ambulance and had him sit down. The second paramedic slipped a blood pressure cuff on his arm, while the first shined a light in his eyes.

"What's going on?" he demanded.

"Mr. Shaw, do I have permission to draw your blood for a drug screen?" Paramedic Number Two asked.

"Hold on." He pulled his arm away.

The cop grabbed him hard enough to make him wince. "There is no baby down there, Mr. Shaw."

George relaxed and smiled. "You probably didn't go far enough. It's a ways in there."

"I've looked." The cop held him with his intense blue eyes. "There is nobody down there."

"They're probably hiding. They'll come out for me."

"Will you allow the paramedic to draw your blood?" the cop asked again.

"Look here, Officer"—he read the name tag on the cop's shirt—"Sullivan. You can have as much blood as you want after you let me show you where they are."

The cop seemed to think that over. After conferring with Paramedic Number One, the cop nodded his head. "Okay. But I'll need to cuff you."

"What for?" George yelled.

"Right now, you're in some serious trouble for reporting a fraudulent medical emergency. I am taking you into custody if you don't cooperate."

"Fine." George stood, turned, and placed his hands behind his back, willing to do anything to get help for the mother and baby.

Both the cop and Number One were armed with intensely bright LED flashlights, which they swept back and forth as they escorted George through the cellar, one on each side with a hand on his biceps.

George wasted no time, moving quickly to where he'd delivered Jeremiah Johnson, only to stop abruptly. "Ruby, come out. It's okay. These people want to help you." He turned around in a circle. "They should be right here. I'm certain. There was a pile of straw. The guy had a lantern. There." He motioned with his head. "My tape measure and clipboard." He stared into the distance, and a cold sweat bathed his face. Panic, fear, and confusion all fought for space in his brain. There was no sign of the woman, her baby, or the man. "It was here. I know it was. Right here." He stamped his foot on the dirt floor.

"Let's keep looking, shall we?" Number One suggested.

"This isn't happening," George muttered. "Where could they have gone? They were here. I saw them, touched them."

Sullivan and Number One patiently walked him around the cellar until they arrived back at the steps. Above ground, there were now two additional patrol cars. Sullivan and Number One were slowly shaking their heads as they talked to the new cops who'd arrived. Another officer took notes and nodded as Shari O'Brien talked and gesticulated wildly.

Sullivan removed George's cuffs from one wrist and sat him down on the rear of the ambulance again. "Do you remember our deal, Mr. Shaw?"

He held out his arm, and Number Two drew his blood.

"How do you feel?" Sullivan asked.

"It was so real. I-I held the baby in my hands." George held his hands out to show them. They were clean.

"Have you been drinking, Mr. Shaw?"

George rolled his eyes. "Of course not. It's only nine o'clock, for God's sake."

"Are you using any other substances?"

"No."

Officer Sullivan pinned him with a hard stare. "How about prescription drugs? Are you taking anything? Maybe you're having a bad reaction to—"

"Nothing." He stared down at his feet and smelled fear oozing from his pores.

"The medics are going to take you to the hospital to get you checked out."

"Sure. I guess."

Sullivan put the cuffs back on, in front this time and very loosely. "Procedure. I'll meet you at the hospital."

George allowed Number Two to guide him into the ambulance. He lay on the stretcher and was strapped in.

Sullivan hung around the hospital until the drug screen came back negative. Then he wished George luck and left to do paperwork. After George was admitted, every doctor in the tristate area came in and asked him the same questions. In between, they ordered tests—blood work, X-rays, and now he was sliding into a tube for a brain scan.

Around midnight, they finally left him alone. He studied the ceiling. *I blew that job. The work was as good as mine; she said as much. It would have carried us through the winter, and I blew it.* He was still awake when the sun came up. Around eight a.m., a doctor he didn't recognize came into his room with a wheelchair.

"Good morning, Mr. Shaw. I'm Dr. Hammond. Hop in. We're going for breakfast."

In the cafeteria, they ate and talked about everything except his experience from the previous day. After multiple cups of coffee, Dr. Hammond wheeled him through the hospital until they reached the doctor's office, a fancy walnut-paneled room. George read the diplomas on the wall for the doctor's work in psychiatry.

"Make yourself comfortable, George."

"Sure. The couch is for me, I guess."

"Sit anywhere you like. You can take the chair behind my desk if you please."

He shrugged but chose a comfortable-looking armchair.

The doctor selected its twin and sat facing him. "I've been over all of your tests, consulted with the doctors who poked and prodded you yesterday. The truth is we can't find anything that would explain your episode."

"So the consensus is I'm crazy."

"There are many things that can trigger a psychotic

episode, although I've never heard one quite like yours before. Are you under a lot of stress?"

"No more than the usual."

"You run a small remodeling business; is that right?"

"Close enough. I specialize in period restorations of old buildings."

"Could it be related to your work?"

"Maybe. Things are looking a little bleak for the winter. But Doc, yesterday I would have sworn to you I delivered a baby in that basement. Today it sounds unbelievable to me too."

Dr. Hammond made some notes on a legal pad. "I'm going to release you. I'd like to see you next week to make sure the medical guys haven't missed anything. Does that sound like something you can do?"

George nodded. "Sure. Does it get me out of here?"

"I'll have you out before they serve lunch." The doctor moved to his desk and consulted an appointment book. "Does next Tuesday at 2:45 work for you?"

George nodded. "Sure."

The doctor handed over a business card with the appointment scrawled in the dreaded doctor script. "Call my office if you have another episode. In the meantime, try not to worry too much. If it is stress related, worrying will only exacerbate your condition."

George recognized the address on the business card. It was an old textile mill recently converted into luxury office condominiums. He knew the developer and the general contractor. He grimaced. Steel studs, drywall, and drop ceilings covered stately stonewalls, yellow pine flooring, and open oak beams, all in the name of maximum return on investment.

Dr. Hammond held the phone to his ear. "Can you send in an aide to take Mr. Shaw back to his room?"

"I can walk."

"Sorry, George, hospital policy. Zero falls and all that."

"And I'll be out of here by lunch?"

"That's a promise. No one should have to stay for any more meals than absolutely necessary."

Back in his room, George found his clothes and dressed. He grabbed his cell phone to make a call, but he had no signal. That little thought had him reliving the events of the day before. *Was it only yesterday?* It seemed long ago and far away. He considered that a good thing. Maybe it would disappear into the vacuum of his mind, the place things go when there is no more room in the file cabinet.

He stopped at the nurse's station and held his cell phone in the air. "I need to check voice mail."

She pointed in a general direction. "Follow the signs for the atrium."

In the atrium, he checked his messages. There was one from his bowling partners. He'd missed last night. They would be pissed if they'd had to forfeit a match on his account. *What the hell am I going to tell them? Sorry, guys, but I had an episode.* Two calls were from his crew leader. He could wait. And finally, there were a half dozen messages from Shari O'Brien. *What is that about?* He had blown that job. His finger unintentionally brushed the call-back button, and the phone started to ring.

Shari picked up on the first ring. "Shari O'Brien."

"This is George Shaw from Blue—"

"Oh my God, George, how are you?"

"I'm good. They're releasing me now."

"I'll pick you up."

He absently scratched his head. That was not the response he'd expected. "That's not necessary."

"Someone wants to meet you. How about I set up lunch?"

"I'd rather get my truck and go home for a shower."

"I understand. He'll be disappointed. I'm leaving now. I'll pick you up out front." The line went dead. She had sounded happier to talk to him today than she had yesterday, before he'd made a mess of things.

A dumpy middle-aged nurse approached him, armed with an iPad and a wheelchair. "Mr. Shaw, you're supposed to be in your room. I need you to sign some forms." She tapped the screen on her iPad and scrolled to the bottom.

"What am I signing?"

"This one says that you are who you say you are."

He signed.

"This one says that you will pay us."

He signed.

"This one is an affidavit swearing that I provided the best possible care during your stay."

He paused and looked at her name tag. "Should I put Edna in here somewhere?"

She smiled. "I've already taken care of that."

He signed.

"You're a free man, Mr. Shaw, unless you stiff us on the payment. In that event, I will visit you at home in the middle of the night. It won't be pleasant."

He laughed. "Thank you, Edna, for providing a level of care eclipsing my demanding expectations."

"Get in, Mr. Shaw." She pushed the wheelchair toward his ankles. "Flattery won't pay the rent."

Edna passed him off to another aide, who delivered him to the front door. He stepped into a brisk fall afternoon with a low ceiling of gunmetal-gray clouds. A horn blew, and Shari O'Brien pulled up.

He slid into her Lexus. "This is very nice of you, but—"

"Nonsense." She wheeled out of the driveway.

"Where are you going? My truck is the other way."

"We're stopping by to see Mr. Johnson first."

"The lawyer? What for? I'm not in any shape to meet anyone right now. Are you suing me or something?"

She laughed. "Nothing is wrong, and we're not suing. I can appreciate how you're feeling. Honestly, I told him we were going to have to find someone else for the project, but he insists on having you. He told me in a very convincing way to get you in his office as soon as possible."

George's mind raced. If he could pull himself together, maybe he could salvage the job. He turned and looked out the window. That was when he realized how fast she was driving.

"I don't get it. Are you sure you've never met him?" Shari asked. "I mean after yesterday's…"

"*Episode*. That's what they called it in the hospital. My episode."

"When I told Mr. Johnson what had happened, he got a little tense and told me to get a hold of you. I thought he might go to the hospital himself."

Now they were driving down the narrow one-way streets of Doylestown. She expertly parallel parked in front of a beautiful old brownstone. The shingle read *Johnson, Johnson, and Johnson, Attorneys at Law*.

Shari got out of the car and waited on the walk. "Are you coming?"

George reluctantly followed her. Even in his current state of agitation, he couldn't pass up a chance to admire Shari's legs as she mounted the steps.

A tall, handsome black man met them at the door and ushered them inside. "You must be George Shaw." He extended his hand and gave George's an energetic shake. "Shari, thank you so much. I'll see that Mr. Shaw gets home."

George recognized the expression on her face before she could recover. He'd gotten the same one yesterday after emerging from the cellar. "Thoroughly pissed" best described it.

"Are you sure, Jeremiah?"

"Absolutely. I'll call you later." He opened the door for her. "Everything is fine. Take the afternoon off."

George steadied himself with a hand on the door-frame. Shari was saying something he didn't hear. The name Jeremiah Johnson echoed in his head. *This shit isn't happening. It doesn't happen, never happens to me. Oh God, not another episode.* He felt for the shrink's card in his shirt pocket. He hoped he could hold off until next Tuesday. The thought of calling that number filled him with dread.

"Mr. Shaw?" Mr. Johnson gave his shoulder a gentle shake. "Are you feeling okay?"

"Yeah, sure." He turned his attention to the big man. "I'm tired is all. I didn't get much sleep in the hospital."

"I understand. Please forgive our insistence on meeting with you. My father is very anxious to talk with you." Mr. Johnson indicated that George should follow him down the hall. He led the way then stopped, rapped on the door, and opened it. "Dad, Mr. Shaw is here." He pushed the door open, led George in, and closed it. "Mr. Shaw, this is my father, Jerry."

An elderly black man with silver hair came around his desk, grasped George's hand in both of his, and shook it. "It is very nice to meet you, Mr. Shaw. Please have a seat." He indicated an overstuffed leather couch.

George took a seat, and the man sat next to him. Jeremiah took a seat in a matching chair opposite them.

"Can I get you anything?" the older man asked. "Water, coffee, scotch, something in between?"

"No, thank you, Mr. Johnson."

"My father is Mr. Johnson. Call me Jerry, please."

"Okay, Jerry, why am I here?"

"Why don't I get right to it? After hearing the crazy story from Shari yesterday, I called in more than a few favors and obtained transcripts of your statements to the police and hospital staff. Be assured, I didn't get any of your medical records. Your story, strange though it was, stayed consistent throughout."

"How does that concern you?"

"You told Officer Sullivan you delivered a baby for Ruby Johnson, who, in turn, named the baby Jeremiah. You no doubt have noticed the fact that it is my son's name as well as my own." He pointed at the brass nameplate on his desk.

"Hard to miss that little fact after the last thirty-six hours."

"What you cannot know is that my great-great-grand-mother's name was Ruby. We know that she escaped slavery with a man assumed to be my great-great-grandfa-ther. We know very little about him, but Mama Ruby gave birth to her first son at the Hood plantation and stayed on there until her death. She named the baby Jeremiah after her father, who died in slavery. The young Jeremiah was the first in my family to be born a free man. What followed was a tradition of naming our firstborn sons Jeremiah."

George's world seemed to be swirling like a tempest. "I'll take that scotch now." He groped for firm ground to stand on.

"JJ, pour us all one, will you please?"

The younger Mr. Johnson got up and went to an armoire. "How do you like your scotch, Mr. Shaw?"

"In a glass. And call me George."

Jerry laughed. "In a glass. That's good, hey, JJ? I guess drinking twenty-five-year-old single malt out of the bottle in a brown paper bag is gauche."

George nodded. "It's just not done."

Jerry smiled. "So you see, George, you witnessed the birth of my great-grandfather yesterday."

George accepted the glass from JJ and took a healthy swallow. "That doesn't seem to surprise you."

"Surprise, no. I'm stupefied." Jerry placed a hand on George's knee. "However, I've had a head start on you, I'm afraid. You no doubt wondered why we were determined to have you for this project."

"The subject came up."

"It was your company name and logo, George. How did you come to name your firm Blue Moon?"

He shrugged. "It sounded better than George Shaw Restoration."

"Over the past thirty-six hours, I've had to reconcile some difficult facts with a family legend handed down orally through the years." Jerry sipped his scotch. "So tell me, George, do you think you saw a ghost yesterday?"

"I don't know what I saw. Maybe you think I'm nuts too, but when I handed that baby boy to his mother, it felt as real as sitting here feels." George emptied his glass and let the alcohol warm his throat.

"I don't think you're nuts. Neither can I explain what happened to you. Was it some kind of time travel? Did you simply witness an event that took place in that basement a long time ago? Did you see the ghost of my great-great-grandmother?" He nodded to his son.

JJ lifted a large garment box from the desk and set it on the coffee table in front of his father.

Jerry continued. "I consider myself an educated man, George, not given to flights of fancy or of great imagination. But there are forces at work here I cannot explain away." He lifted the lid off the box and slid the container in front of George.

Inside, a very old and well-used denim jacket was preserved in a vacuum-sealed bag. Something embroidered on the left breast caught George's attention. A full moon crossed by a claw hammer above the words Blue Moon Restoration.

The Deadly Trees Of Cape Blanco

What I'm about to tell you, you will no doubt find absurd. For that reason, I've resisted telling the story for seventy-eight years. No one would have believed it. They would have just branded me a liar. To go through life labeled a liar would have certainly been awful. What happened instead is far worse. I beg a God I don't believe in to take my life because living in an asylum is not a life.

We have caregivers at the hospital—doctors, nurses, and attendants—who are here to help us. The lie they tell is that they are trying to make us well. The truth is no one leaves here standing up. Caregiver, according to my dog-eared paperback dictionary, is defined as a paid helper who regularly looks after a child or a person who is sick, elderly, or disabled. There is more looking away than looking after in this place. It is more like off-site storage, where unseemly items are moved to wait out a predetermined sentence before being disposed of. I am *provided* meals, if you want to call them that, for they barely meet the requirements of sustenance. My caretakers are more concerned with ensuring I swallow the medications that make me no healthier, just easier to manage.

Having outlived most everyone I've ever known—anyone of importance, that is—I have no visitors. Sometimes I get visits from well-meaning folks that come hoping to raise the spirits of those of us who for the most part have been forgotten. Some bring dogs. Those are the best days, but they are infrequent, and their visits are far too short. One of those well-meaning folks gave me the composition book I'm writing in now, along with this pen, which has sparkles and unicorns on the barrel. I felt a little silly writing with such a pen at first, but once you've read this, it may make a certain kind of sense.

I doubt very much anyone will be interested in the meandering reminiscences of an old man. Once I'm gone, my meager possessions will be packed up. When they realize no one will be claiming my things, or my remains for that matter, it will all get thrown in some landfill. I can only hope the landfill will someday be repurposed and my things will become the foundation of a playground where thirteen-year-old boys and girls can play without fear.

In truth, I'm not writing this for anyone to read. I hope by this confession I may get some relief in my last days on this earth.

I seem to have digressed from the story. You'll have to forgive an old man. My concentration isn't what it used to be.

Even at thirteen years of age, I knew enough to keep my mouth shut and let the adults form a narrative they could live with. I would not speak and feigned no memory of the weekend my class set out to visit the most western point of Oregon. But in truth, I will never forget the trip to Cape Blanco. Not a single bloody detail will ever fade from my memory. Not a day goes by that I don't think about my friends and teachers who perished there. Not a night passes that I don't wake up in a pool of sweat, my mouth stretched wide in a silent scream. I haven't used my voice since that day. In the beginning, I chose to remain mute. The longer I went without speaking, the easier it became. I don't think I could utter a sound now if I wanted to.

It was late spring of 1940. Our teachers were running out of time to grind knowledge into our young minds. After the long winter, we had little interest in what they were trying to teach. I gazed out the window, watching the trees leaf out in the sun. I was not alone. A field trip had been rumored, but few details leaked. An excursion to some exotic location was the perfect remedy for our lack of focus.

Finally, it happened. Permission slips were sent home, accompanied by an explanation of where we would be going and a plea for volunteers to assist as chaperones.

The plan was for us to camp in tents in the woods on Cape Blanco, visit the lighthouse, and learn the history of blah, blah, blah. Who cared—we were going camping.

"Camping!" I said to my mom. "We're going camping?"

"I'm not so sure about this." She looked over her glasses. "Who will—"

"Not sure about what?"

"Don't interrupt me, or you won't be going anywhere, young man. I have to stay home with Brittany. I won't be able to help chaperone. Who's going to keep an eye on you?"

"There will be teachers and other moms and dads. Come on, I gotta go."

"You don't 'gotta' go. What are they teaching you at

that school if you 'gotta' do anything?" She waved the permission slip at me.

"Sorry. But I really, really, really, *really* want to go, Mom. Please." My voice cracked on the please.

"Let me make a call."

"Who you gonna… Who are you going to call?" I corrected myself.

"Let me check with Mr. Overby. If he's going *and* he agrees to keep an eye on you, then I think I can come up with the money."

"Thanks, Mom." Spontaneously, I hugged her. It was in the bag. Clarence Overby was my best friend. His dad would never say no. He often said it was easy to find Clarence because he was always with me. Mrs. Overby would add that it was easier to find me because I practically lived at their house. "Can I go tell Clarence the good news?"

"Mr. Overby hasn't agreed yet," she reminded me. "You don't even know if Clarence is going."

"Yeah. I mean yes. I'll ask." I was out the door and through the hedge separating our houses in a flash.

Over the next couple of weeks, we learned the history of the Oregon lighthouses that dotted the coastline and why it was necessary to ship goods by sea because of the lack of roads. We were enthralled by descriptions of the tragic wrecks that took place on the rocky shoals of Oregon and by all the reasons the lighthouses were so important to settling the northwest coast. We learned about the hardships of the keepers and their families, who lived in those remote outposts and kept the lights burning.

Clarence and I read everything we could get our hands on about living in the wild. Jack London was our favorite. His story, *To Build A Fire*, chilled us to the bone. We practiced building fires every weekend until that magical

Saturday arrived when we boarded the school bus to travel west.

When we arrived on the coast, I was stunned by the ferocious wind. Cape Blanco jutted out into the Pacific Ocean. The wind got a running start in Canada and collided with its first speed bump at Cape Blanco. It sculpted everything it touched. Trees were misshapen into distorted, cartoonish figures. Dunes were created, blown away, and recreated. Waves crashed on the rocks, grinding them to sand.

After the tour of the lighthouse, we retreated to the camping area, which was tucked into an old-growth pine forest. The wind rushed by over our heads, but we were spared the pummeling we'd experienced on the bluff. The roar, however, was relentless. The treetops thrashed, and the noise seemed unendurable. Some said it would die down soon, while others said we would get used to it. Mr. Overby was in the you'll-get-used-to-it camp.

The adults started the fire over the objections of Clarence and me. We offered to do it, but they weren't having it. Dinner was comprised of beans and franks. It was starting out to be the best weekend ever. Several of us decided to explore the woods. We were warned not to wander too far, to be back before dark, and not to go alone. "Too far" meant nothing to a group of thirteen-year-old boys. So Georgie, Bobby, Clarence, and I set out for parts unknown.

We wandered through the pines until we came to a thick copse of strange-looking trees. Twisted trunks with giant limbs reached for us. The branches were entwined, making the trees easier to climb through than to walk around. The rough bark caught at our clothes and shoes as we ventured deeper. We climbed until the wind grasped at us, then we descended, moving in no general direction.

When someone yelped and cursed, I knew it wasn't Clarence, so I paid little heed until he called out to me. Heaving a big sigh I hoped he couldn't hear over the wind, I worked my way back to where the other boys were gathered. Georgie's calf was gashed a good one and bleeding pretty heavily by the time I reached the rest of the group.

"What?" I asked.

"Watch this, Curt," Clarence said. "Do it, Georgie."

Georgie shifted his position, pushing his bleeding leg against a tree limb. When he pulled it away, it was clean. I could plainly see the depth of the cut until the blood seeped out, blurring the wound again.

I shrugged. "So?"

"The tree soaks up the blood like a sponge," Georgie explained.

"You wiped it off on the tree."

"Did not," Georgie said.

"Get out. Are you guys falling for this manure?" I started away.

"Show him again," Clarence said.

"You do it," Georgie said.

"I'm not doing it." Clarence shook his head. "Not no way, not no how."

"Are you afraid?" Bobby chimed in.

I pointed a challenging finger at Bobby's chest. "You do it if you're so brave. I dare you."

"Fine." He pulled a Barlow pocketknife out and proceeded to slice a shallow cut across the fingerprint of his thumb. Blood welled up and dripped onto the ground. He placed his cut against the tree then pulled it away. His finger was clean. The bark absorbed the blood like a gauze pad.

I remained skeptical, so when his cut welled up again, I stepped in closer. "Let me hold your thumb."

Bobby shrugged and held out his hand. I guided it to a different branch and pressed it for a one-one thousand count and pulled it away. It was clean. I whistled my astonishment.

Bobby held out his Barlow. "You want to try it?"

"No, thanks. I'm not feeding these trees my blood."

Bobby thrust the knife at me handle first. "I double dare you."

A double dare couldn't be refused. I took the knife and repeated Bobby's action, slicing my thumb. Clarence followed me. We stood around in awe, watching the blood disappear from our various wounds.

Georgie interrupted, his voice sounding weak. "Hey, guys." He pointed down at his leg.

A small branch had wrapped itself around his leg over his injury. It nuzzled in as though holding on. I nudged it with my foot. It didn't move.

Georgie made a show of pulling away, but the branch held firm. "Get it off me." Panic laced his voice.

We bent to the task, but the branch might as well have been made of iron. Bobby brandished his Barlow and attempted to saw through it. When he cut into the bark, pink sap dripped from the scar. We gasped as one when we saw it. Bobby doubled his efforts to cut through the branch.

Georgie's face was pale. "Hurry, Bobby. Get it off."

That was when I noticed another branch snaking around Bobby's ankle. I stomped on it. "Clarence, go get help. Tell them to bring a hatchet." I returned my attention to the vine-like thing reaching for Bobby's ankle. It moved slowly, but it moved. I became aware of my own arms and legs. The trees got faster and stronger the longer we struggled with them. Some branches were attached to

George's other leg now. When I looked up, Clarence was staring at my feet. "Go," I shouted. "Run!"

He bolted away. It was the last time I ever saw him alive. Light was fading. We screamed for help, but no one came. Georgie wasn't saying anything. I tapped Bobby on the shoulder and pointed. Georgie's face was translucent. His sunken eyes stared at nothing. "Let's get out of here," I said.

Bobby shook his head. "I'm not leaving him here."

My voice climbed an octave. "Come on."

"I'm not leaving him."

I wrapped my arms around Georgie and tried to drag him away. His body was light. Too light. But I could only get him so far because more branches were entwined around him now. When I stopped pulling, he collapsed in my arms. "Bobby, we gotta go."

Bobby joined me. "Hold on. Let's pull together."

I held Georgie under his arms, and Bobby grasped him around the waist. Together, we pulled until the muscles in our stringy arms quivered with the effort. I panted from the exertion.

Bobby shouted, "Keep going! We almost had him."

The vines were thicker than ever. "Bobby, it's too late. He's a goner."

Bobby persisted. "On the count of three."

We pulled together, but nothing happened. Another vine crept up my leg. I dropped Georgie and jumped back. "He's dead. Can't you see that?"

Bobby looked up at me with terror in his eyes. The trees had fastened on him while we tried to free Georgie.

"Help me," Bobby said through gritted teeth.

I tugged at the creepers. They writhed in my grip. Disgusted, I jerked away. "I can't. They're too strong." Another wrapped around my arm. I jumped to my feet, emitting a scream. The trees grew more aggressive.

Bobby's eyes pleaded with me to stay, but he didn't speak again. The vines continued to noiselessly wrap themselves around him. They crept higher and higher, tightening their grip. His struggles waned, and he grew pale. I could see it was too late for him.

Blindly, I ran, lashing out at anything that touched me. Screams tore from my throat. I ran like only a thirteen-year-old boy could run, tripping over roots, crashing into branches, and falling on my face. But still, I ran. In the distance, I heard screams. But they faded with every step I put between those trees and me.

Seventy-eight years later, I am still haunted by Bobby's eyes. I will die soon. Actually, I'm looking forward to it. Then I may finally escape the terrors that visit me every night. And when that day finally arrives, I'll have to answer for leaving Bobby. Remembering his face, I hope that seeing those eyes all these years will be punishment enough. Some people fear Hell. After reliving that day in my nightmares, I don't think Hell could be any worse.

Fear was a powerful motivator. That night, fear drove me until my legs betrayed me. They gave out, quivering like jelly beneath me, and I slammed into the ground. It was dark. There was no moon or stars, just the distant beacon of the lighthouse, passing overhead. The unrelenting wind tore at my clothes. It howled its lament, sounding like forty voices. I huddled there, waiting for death to come. With hands clamped against my ears, I lay with my face pressed to the ground and cried myself to sleep.

I awoke in the gray of predawn, lying in a pasture, shivering. Sheep grazed in the distance. The lighthouse beam cut through the early morning mist. Using it as a reference, I made my way to the road then followed it to where we had parked the bus. The sun was up by then, and I unzipped my jacket as I walked to our camp. Not a living soul stirred. I walked around the campsite, lifting tent flaps, and I soon realized they'd all left. From what I could tell, all our supplies remained.

Embers glowed in the firepit. I pocketed a box of large kitchen matches and slowly followed the same path my friends and I had taken the night before. When I reached the grove of prehistoric trees, I saw something in the distance dangling from the branches. Afraid to go any closer, I walked along the edge until I realized what I was seeing. Strewn around the ancient trees were clothes. It looked like my room at home before Mom would threaten to send me to school naked if I didn't pick up. The sight made no sense, yet it disturbed me. I dared to go a little closer. When I did, I recognized Mr. Overby's jacket, cap, and shriveled face. Clinging to his sleeve, my best friend, Clarence, hung like a deflated balloon. A moan escaped my lips, and I retched. These weren't just clothes. My friends were hanging in the trees, sucked dry. The currents of wind that dipped low into the forest animated what was left of their exsanguinated bodies as if they were scarecrows.

That was where my memory got sketchy. Overcome with grief and rage, I blindly labored all day, carrying dry tinder and grass to the edge of the deadly grove of trees. In spite of my attempts to do otherwise, I couldn't keep my eyes off the macabre scene before me. Bodies were draped in the trees like Halloween decorations. I built a large pile of fuel as tall as me and about ten feet long at the edge of the trees.

The sun had moved to the western horizon. My clothes were covered in dirt and patches of dried grass. Pine needles clung to my sweaty face. Muscles ached, but I couldn't say I noticed. Crouched on the ground, using my body to shield the flame from the wind, I broke the first few matchsticks. My hands shook, and tears blurred my vision. I finally struck a spark. The sulfur smoke stung my nose. Carefully, I nursed the small flame to health. I fed it dry tinder and grass. Gradually, I coaxed the fire to catch. As the minutes passed, the flames grew in spite of the tears temporarily quenching the fuel. The wind became my friend, feeding huge gulps of oxygen to the hungry fire. It burned hot, and the wind wailed over the snapping of larger pieces of wood starting to ignite.

The heat became intense. Steam rose from my clothes. I backed away a step and watched the blaze gain momentum as it moved through the grove of ancient trees where I'd left my friends to die. The wind shrieked, and the trees howled.

It was dark before the volunteer fire department arrived. They put me in an ambulance and delivered me to a nearby hospital. I was treated for second-degree burns and smoke inhalation. In the days and weeks that followed, only one explanation seemed to make sense to the officials. I refused to speak. I had left my friends to die. I deserved to be punished. So when they asked if I had started the fire, I nodded. Eventually, I was moved to the Blanco County Hospital for the criminally insane.

The name has changed several times over the years, but the facility hasn't. It has been my home for seventy-eight years. During my stay, I have researched every kind of tree known to mankind. Thankfully, I have never found anything like the ones I destroyed that spring day in 1940. I will spend my remaining days, may they be few, wondering what freak of nature took the lives of my classmates.

Shadowman

Ted pulled off the blacktop surface onto a dirt track. He stopped and shifted the Jeep into four-wheel drive. The trail he sought would be difficult to find in the dark, so he proceeded slowly. After consulting a trail map, he found it. *What the hell am I doing? I know better than to head into the desert in August.*

Of course the desert was a key component of his plan. He would hike until his water ran out. That way, if he lost his nerve, the desert would finish the job for him. And no one would be around to interfere. *It doesn't really matter where I end it all, as long as I don't fuck it up. I need to stop the pain. Get off the hamster wheel. Why do we struggle to survive another day when the next day brings the same shit in spades?*

The Jeep Wrangler he'd always wanted crept along under the predawn sky, following the trail past cactus and sagebrush. *Who the hell will even miss me? Not the siblings I never talk to. Or the friends I don't have. Work associates are what I have, and they'll just say, "Hey, did you hear about Ted?"* He knew the husbands of his wife's friends, but they weren't his friends. *My wife will be upset, but in truth, she'll be better off without me.*

His body reflexively drove, while his brain remained otherwise occupied.

On the horizon, a sliver of light appeared, pulling him away from his justification. The skyline lit up orange against the dark-blue background. *The sun will be here soon. That's when the waste matter encounters the rotating air circulator.* In the northern edge of the Sonoran Desert, the daytime temperature could reach 115 degrees on a clear day in August.

He slipped on his sunglasses as he drove in the direction of the rising sun. It soon crested the horizon in all its unforgiving glory. The track he'd been following had disappeared some miles back, and now he picked his way across the desert floor, doing as little damage as possible. With the terrain getting increasingly rocky, he stopped to take a look around. He took a moment to quench his thirst, when the urgent need to piss hit him. He climbed out of the jeep, stretched, and relieved himself. *This is the perfect metaphor for my life. You pour it in one end and let it out the other. Nothing much happens in the middle. I'm going through the motions of life without actually living. Well, all that's about to change.* He put on a hat and checked his pack. He had six liters of water, a half dozen power bars, two liters of Captain Morgan's finest rum, a sleeping bag, and his Sig. He struck out on foot for the foothills.

Hours later, he stumbled and landed on his ass. The sun was at its zenith, and the way had gotten progressively steeper. The jolt of the fall snapped his mouth shut, and he bit the inside of his cheek. Sitting there, a little dazed and tasting blood, he started to giggle. The giggle turned into a laugh that shook his whole body. He noticed a large rock at the edge of the incline. It looked as if it could roll down the side of the mountain at any minute. It would take no prisoners when it decided to do just that. It formed a small pocket of shade on the downhill side, and Ted took advantage of it. In the shade of the benevolent rock, he drew the tepid water from the bladder in his pack. Heat and exhaustion put him to sleep in short order.

When he awoke, the sun sat on the western horizon. He got up with a start, but the stiffness in his back and legs put him back down. Moaning, he stretched a little and stood up more slowly. *This isn't the right place. I need to get a move on. It's only two steps. One, two, one, two, and so it goes.* The sun and low clouds combined to paint as beautiful a sunset as Ted could remember. He couldn't recall the last time he'd actually watched a sunset. All of his adult life, he'd thought things like sunsets were frivolous. *It happens every day. What's the big deal?*

He realized he'd left his hat at the rock. *I won't need it again.* He unwrapped his last power bar and walked toward the ridge. At the top, he looked around. In the distance, he spied a grouping of mesquite trees hovering above scrubby Green Cloud sage bushes. "Promising," he said.

With a destination in sight, a little spring returned to his step. The light played with the shadows around the trees. He made a point of not watching his feet as Mother Nature performed act two of her daily theater solely for Ted's enjoyment.

The twilight faded as he walked into the little oasis. The view of the valley that lay at his feet took his breath away. He drank the rest of his water and threw down his pack. The beautiful panorama held his gaze until the light faded to black. Then he scavenged for firewood. He spread out his sleeping bag and sat down for the second time in twelve hours. The fire caught, and the flames pushed the darkness back a bit. Outside his small circle of light, the black grew intense. The firelight made him blind to what lay beyond, and that unsettled him. He opened the rum and took a hearty swallow.

The burn made him wince. *That's a rough way to start drinking after fifty-three weeks of sobriety.* He'd been trying to stop for three years and a week. After taking a one-year medallion, he'd given up. He'd hung on the best he could, but his misery always got the best of him. In the end, it would have its way. *I've made my peace with it. I'm done.*

Removing the Sig from his pack, Ted felt the weight and balance of the handgun. It was a good-looking piece. He had a Glock at home, but it lacked style. He'd decided it was too pedestrian for the job he had in mind. *Now this has a sense of beauty and purpose.* The website he'd purchased it from had called it sexy. He wasn't sure he would go that far. The Sig Sauer P226 MK25 was the handgun preferred by the Navy SEALs, and that made it more than suitable for the night's mission. Tonight, it would serve a final call of duty.

Taking another long pull from the bottle of rum, Ted heard a noise. Hastily, he stood, getting a little head rush in the process, and listened.

"Didn't mean to startle you there, young fella. It's just that I don't get many visitors out here." The voice sounded like gravel sliding down a wooden chute. Ted's heart raced when a tall figure stepped into the light cast by his camp-fire. *How long has he been out there, watching me?*

"I wouldn't mind a sip of that there hooch if you could spare a little." The old man extended his hand toward Ted. "I reckon my manners have slipped some, what with being out here alone most of the time. Name's Mitch, but folks mostly call me Shadowman."

Ted realized the stranger's hand waited in midair. He shook the offered hand. The man had a solid handshake, a working man's hand for sure. "Sorry, I… uh, well, I thought you might be an illusion at first. Nice to meet you." Ted swept out his arm as if welcoming somebody into his home. "Pull up a piece of desert and help yourself to a drink. I'm afraid I can't offer you a glass."

As Mitch squatted down on his haunches, he picked up the bottle, wiped the top with his dirty shirtsleeve, and took a big swallow. "That'll kick your ass when you don't partake in the devil's brew much." Mitch hefted the bottle up and took another swig. "It goes down a little too easy. Here's to new friends, then." He passed the bottle over to Ted.

"To new friends." Ted took a sip.

"Well, Ted, folks don't come out here to make new friends, so if I'm wearing out my welcome, you just say so."

Ted hesitated. *Did I tell him my name? No, I didn't. But I must have.* "I have to say, I certainly didn't expect to have company tonight."

"Don't imagine you did. It doesn't look like you plan on staying long either."

"What makes you say that?"

"I don't want to be rude, but you don't strike me as a guy who can survive long in the desert on your wits, and you didn't bring many provisions. I mean, what I'm seeing —a jug of hooch, a sleeping bag, and that pea shooter— won't keep you alive very long out here."

"Well, you're right, Mitch. I'm just passing through." *Passing on is more accurate.* "Are there any more folks around here? I walked most of the day and didn't see a soul. Then right out of nowhere, you walk up as if I'm standing in the checkout line of a Circle K." Ted passed the bottle back.

"I'd say you just got lucky, or unlucky, depending on your point of view. There isn't another soul for hundreds of square miles. You know, this stuff will kill you on an empty stomach." Mitch took another drink. "I've got some beans and coffee. Why don't you come over to my place? Have a bite to eat." He handed the bottle back.

Ted smiled genuinely this time. "This stuff will kill you on a full stomach too." *And that is the whole point.* "I think I have to pass, but thanks for the offer."

"I'm sorry to hear that. I could sure use a little company tonight."

"I've got some things I need to think on."

"Whatever you're doing out here can wait a couple hours, can't it? Enough time for an old geezer to exercise his vocal cords."

Ted's resolve weakened. "How far is it? I'm not in much shape for a long trek." *This codger is throwing a wrench in my plan.*

"Just over there." Mitch raised his arm and vaguely pointed off to his right. "Not far. You lean on old Mitch." He offered Ted a hand up.

"I guess I've got time for a dish of beans." Ted took the offered hand and staggered as he stood.

"Steady as she goes. It's just up ahead a piece." Mitch kept a steadying hand on Ted and still managed to gather Ted's few possessions. Finally, the old man scattered sand across the remains of the fire with his boot. "Here we go, Teddy."

Ted didn't like the nickname Teddy. Even though he usually corrected anyone who used it, he let it slide. Coming from this tall, weathered man with the indistinguishable drawl, it didn't bother him. *I still don't remember telling him my name, though.*

They walked together into the darkness. Ted's unsteady gait did not keep him from recognizing that Mitch's camp was close, very close. What would the bookies in Vegas make of him traveling blindly in the desert for twelve hours and landing on the doorstep of the only living soul for hundreds of square miles? *That's a sucker's bet for sure.*

Mitch's camp was a simple affair but clearly lived in. Paths worn in the hard-packed earth between the campfire and tent indicated as much. A fire glowed inside a ring of stones that supported a rusted metal grate. A dented pot missing its handle sat over the fire. A wisp of steam escaped from the lid, which was also dented. The aroma of real cowboy beans drifted to Ted and made his stomach growl. On the corner of the grate sat an old-fashioned coffee percolator. Mitch untied a rope and lowered a burlap sack that had been hanging high in the tree. He removed two tin mugs and poured dark liquid from the pot into them.

"Try that, my friend. It ain't Starbucks, but it will keep you up until you find one, and it'll grow a little hair on your chest while you're looking." Mitch touched the side of his cup to Ted's.

Ted took a small sip of the brew. "Whoa, that will grow hair on your back too, but it does chase away the chill."

"That there is Coast Guard coffee. I worked off the coast of Maine, saving lost souls. We mostly rescued fishermen trying to scratch out a living in the North Atlantic. That's why I came out here when I got my pension." Mitch looked off into the distance. "Too many memories —ice-cold water; thirty-foot swells washing over the deck; me tied to the railing, searching for the overeager crew of a fishing trawler; the fishermen out there, desperately hunting for home and praying that we get to them in time."

The imagery Mitch created had Ted considering how easily a rescue mission like that could go badly. *What would that feel like?* Stillness held sway over Ted, while Mitch gazed into the darkness.

Breaking the spell, Ted said, "You don't sound like a New Englander."

"Ha ha. No, indeed I'm not, but you don't get to pick where you're going to serve when you sign up. The Guard sends you where you're needed."

"You miss the sea?"

"I get a little homesick for the work. I miss the fishermen, the men I served with. Most of all, I miss the gratitude in the eyes of the wives, sons, daughters, and mothers of the men I helped to bring home."

"That sounds like rewarding work."

"Until I start counting my scars. Some of them you can see, but most are on the inside, where they can only be felt. Wounds that will tear the soul right out of a man. Injuries only the Father can heal. Then I remember why I'm as far away from that she-devil as I can get." He shook his head and spooned generous portions of beans onto tin plates that matched the beat-up cups.

Ted accepted his plate. The steam rising off the beans had Ted salivating. He saw chunks of pork amidst the beans for added flavor.

"A word of thanks before you dig in," Mitch said.

Ted's fork was halfway to his mouth. He set it back on his plate and bowed his head.

"Father, thank you for the feast you have set before us. May we use it wisely. Amen."

Ted muttered, "Amen." In that moment after Mitch's prayer, he heard the desert holding its breath reverently. The beans landed in Ted's empty stomach with a thump, and before he knew what had hit him, he was using his finger to mop up the liquid left on the plate.

"I could say you was a mite hungry there, Teddy."

"I guess I was."

Mitch cleared the plates, poured more coffee, and

topped the cups off with a generous shot of rum. Sitting back, he let out a contented sigh. "Well, Teddy, this has been a very pleasant evening so far. How's about I roll us up a couple smokes?" He dug into the pocket of his dusty overalls and produced a leather pouch.

"I don't smoke."

"You don't drink either, but I see you're indulging yourself tonight. You might as well do it up right. This here is the best tobacco you'll find this side of heaven." Mitch's nimble fingers rolled two of the smoothest-looking hand-rolled smokes Ted had ever seen. They were perfect.

"How do you know I don't drink?"

"You'd be surprised at what I know about you, my friend. Try one of these. This isn't that chemically treated stuff the tobacco companies produce." Mitch lit both cigarettes with a piece of wood from the fire and passed one over.

Ted inhaled deeply. He was shocked he didn't launch into a coughing fit. This was by far the smoothest smoke he'd ever had. Ted felt a little dizzy. "That is one smooth smoke."

"Don't get too used to it. You'll not find it again." Mitch smiled. "For an old man, I guess it doesn't get much better than this."

"You said you know things about me." Ted looked at Mitch intently, trying to figure out if they'd met before and if so, when. "What do you think you know?"

Mitch's eyes reflected the firelight. His face was lined with life's experiences. "Do you want to talk about it?"

Ted tilted his head in confusion. *Maybe it's the rum or the smoke, but this guy is talking in circles.* "Talk about what?"

"Something brought you out here. You're running from something. If you don't want to talk about it, just say so. I can do enough talking for the both of us."

Ted said nothing for a long stretch. The quiet pressed down on him. Mitch held his gaze. "It sounds trite when I say it out loud. So I won't. But you're right. I am running, and I mean to stay ahead of it."

"A blind man can see you mean to take your life with that shooting iron of yours. Did you stop to consider your life might not be yours to take?"

"What the hell does that even mean? Of course it's mine."

"How did you come by it? Did you earn it? Did you make it?"

I'm out of here. Ted stood on shaky legs. "I guess I'll be heading out now. Thanks for the beans and the coffee."

Mitch blinked. "Sit yourself down and relax."

Ted's legs betrayed him, and he landed back on the log.

"I said I could talk for both of us. I didn't say you'd like everything I have to say. That's the way of it. How about if I pour us another cup of joe? You top it off with the secret ingredient and let an old man prattle on."

"I don't know." *I'm not sure I can stand, let alone walk out of here.* "Maybe we can change the subject."

"No one can stop you from doing what you came out here to do, certainly not some old sailor who is half in the bag." Mitch refilled their cups and held them out, waiting for Ted to pour the booze.

Reluctantly, Ted topped off the coffee cups and accepted one. "Here's to fulfilling your destiny."

Mitch clicked his cup against Ted's. "Destiny, very philosophical. Which brings me back to my earlier question. Where did you get your life? Or a better question would be, who gave it to you?"

"That's a pretty good-size pile of wood you have over there. It must have taken a while to collect it."

"Yes, indeed. But I have all the time in the world. How much time do you have?"

"You're not going to let this go, are you?"

Mitch shook his grizzled face. "Not likely."

"Roll two more of those smokes and answer a question for me."

Mitch dug out his tobacco pouch. "Ask away."

"Why do you care what I do with *my* life?"

"That's complicated. But let me try to explain. When I was in the North Atlantic, bobbing around in those storms, what do you think I was doing?" Mitch sealed up two more perfect hand-rolleds and passed one to Ted.

"Your job?"

"I was saving lives. I'd have done anything to bring every one of those men home. But I couldn't save them all. Not a day goes by that I don't think about the ones we lost." Mitch paused. "That's more than a job."

"I get it. You saved those men. But I don't want to be saved. So I'll ask again—why do you care?"

"Because it's not about you. It's not your life to throw away. Doesn't mean you can't do it. It means you shouldn't do it."

"We'll have to agree to disagree on that one." Ted poured more coffee and added the rum. It seemed like the coffeepot should have been empty by then, but it felt near full when he lifted it off the fire. The rum should have been gone by then too, but a fair amount still sloshed in the bottle.

"Just think about it. I guess that's all I'm asking. I believe every man has a purpose."

"That a joke? What purpose can you possibly have, living in the middle of nowhere like a hermit?"

"I know what my purpose is." Mitch sighed. "Do you know yours?"

Ted used a stick from the fire to scratch at the dirt between his boots. *This old codger is getting on my nerves. Who cares what he thinks? Like he said earlier, no one can stop me. Besides, if the bullet doesn't get me, the desert will.*

Mitch cleared his throat. "You don't, do you?"

"Don't what?"

"Have a purpose."

"All I have is pain. The harder I work, the more I succeed, the more miserable I get. So where does it end?"

"I think you're looking in all the wrong places, my friend. Material things aren't the answer."

"What is the answer? All my life, I thought if you work hard and get ahead, your life will get easier."

Mitch let loose a belly laugh. When he caught his breath, he shook his head. "I don't know where you heard that one, but nothing can be further from the truth. Everything you love requires work if you want to keep it. And I don't mean a new Jeep. I mean the stuff that matters. Possessions don't matter. People matter. And people are work. Hard work."

Ted digested that. *How come I feel like I work my ass off, and I don't even have people?*

"Because you're prioritizing the wrong things."

I didn't say that out loud, did I? "Are you reading my mind too?"

"It's not that hard." Mitch rolled two more smokes. "Last one, then I'm hitting the sack."

Ted poured the coffee. "Last call."

"Think about what I said. Give it until tomorrow. But you should know that when that nor'easter comes across your bow, and she will come, she'll be blowing a fair bitch. Lash yourself to the rail and meet her head on. There's no storm you can't weather when you ask for help."

"Help from who? The Coast Guard?"

"No, Ted. The Coast Guard can't help you. It wasn't the Guard that saved those men in the North Atlantic either. We were just tools. You have to find a real source of power. Infinite power."

Ted nodded. He'd heard those words before in an Alcoholics Anonymous meeting. It had never been something he was willing to do. "I'll think about it."

"Good man. That's all I'm asking. Now I'm hitting my bunk. Good night."

"Good night, Mitch. I'll see you in the morning." The night was warm, so Ted rolled out his sleeping bag and lay on top of it. He'd never seen so many stars. The night sky was alive with them. He marveled at the natural beauty and considered the ever-expanding, infinite universe. *There's that word again. Infinite. I can't wrap my head around infinite.* Sleep came slowly, and the sky started to lighten in the east before his eyes closed.

Stiff and groggy, Ted woke with the sun in his eyes. "Where am I?" An empty bottle of rum lay on the ground next to him. The fog in his brain slowly lifted, and the events of the previous day started to come back to him. "I walked out here yesterday. How long have I been sleeping? Where's the old guy?"

Ted sat up and looked around but saw nothing. The old man's camp was gone. He saw the tree the old guy had hung his provisions from, but the rope and sack were nowhere to be found. The ashes from the fire were still warm to the touch, but no stone ring was evident. The tent and the firewood were gone too. He stood, trying to remember details. He could almost hear the old-timer talking in the gravelly drawl. But he couldn't quite remember what the man looked like.

Did I dream all of that? I don't think so. This doesn't make any sense. He picked up his pack to check for the Sig and was surprised by the weight. The water bladders had been refilled. They were both empty the night before. He found the handgun and ejected the clip. It was still loaded. He turned a full circle, looking for any sign of the old man. *He couldn't have packed up and moved. Could he? What the hell is going on?* The sky was clear, and the sun sat low on the western horizon.

Did I sleep the whole day away? Is that possible? He took some deep breaths to get control and kicked the empty two-liter bottle of rum. He felt pretty good for someone who'd drunk all that rum. His mind spun, searching for an explanation as to what had happened last night. Next to the fire, scratched into the hardpack desert terrain, were two words:

WHOSE LIFE

A gravelly voice spoke up in his head. "God's life, that's whose."

I'm still dreaming. Snap out of it. Hand-rolled cigarette butts were scattered about at his feet. He picked one up and examined it. "Shit. If it was a dream, then where did these come from? And if it wasn't a dream, where's the old philosopher?"

He took a moment to get his bearings. The sun kissed the horizon. This was as good a time as any to head back. If he traveled in the cool of the night, he would be home around dawn... if his jeep was still there. He glanced up at the sky. *Will it be there?*

The gravelly voice spoke again. "Of course. It's waiting for a man with a purpose."

I guess you'll tell me what that purpose is when I need to know.

Nightshift

Z ach burst through the swinging doors from the loading dock, shedding his wet coat as he went. In the locker room, he changed into scrubs before he headed to the autopsy theater. The bass line from "My Girl" bled through the lime-green concrete walls of the morgue, answering his first question of the night. *Who will be assisting?* With the Temptations playing loud enough to wake the dead, Marvin would be Zach's attendant, and the twelve-hour shift would pass quickly and painlessly.

The doors to the autopsy room hissed open at Zach's approach. Music exploded through the cold air, bouncing off stainless-steel and ceramic-tile surfaces. Marvin danced across the room, wheeling out a gurney that held their first victim of the evening. He stopped mid-spin. "My man, pots and pans." Marvin pointed his remote at the Bose player and lowered the volume. "Dr. Zach, you better kick off them winter boots and put on your dancing slippers. We celebratin' tonight, so it's gotta be all Temptations, all the time."

"And pray tell, Mr. Gaye, what are we celebrating tonight?"

"Today is the sixth of March, and in 1965, 'My Girl' hit number one on the charts, the same night I lost my virginality." Marvin's gold tooth gleamed in the harsh lighting.

"You mean your virginity, and that's too much information."

Marvin executed a three-hundred-sixty-degree turn with effortless grace. The Temptations moved on to "I'm Losing You."

The wall phone buzzed, indicating a call within the system. At just after midnight, it could only be one person. Marvin lowered the music further.

"What does she want? I just got here." Zach lifted the handset. "This is Morgan."

Amelia bypassed the ritual greeting. "Dr. Morgan, you parked in the visitors' lot again."

"Why does it matter where I park? It's the middle of the night. I don't think we'll be overrun with visitors."

"Regulations specify *all* employees are to park in the designated employee parking lot. There are no exceptions for *doctors* that I'm aware of."

"But it's freezing rain outside."

"Do I have to wake the Chief Medical Examiner at this hour?"

"All right, for Christ's sake, I'll move it." He slammed the handset into the cradle. "She threatened to call the Chief."

Marvin rolled his eyes. "She'd do it too."

Zach turned. "I'll be back."

"Y'all ain't fixin' to do sumpin' stupid?"

"Actually, I am. I'm going out in this god-awful

weather, without a coat, to move my car to the employee parking lot until the Wicked Witch of West Philly finds something else to bitch about."

"I'll get our first Mr. Doe on the table. Doc, you stay away from the second floor."

"You notice her broomstick is parked right next to the door. I should throw a bucket of water on her. Maybe she'll melt."

"I know yo mama didn't raise no fools. Besides, we celebratin' tonight."

Zach raised his right hand. "No second floor."

Zach returned from the employee parking lot, shivering. Sterilized instruments lay scattered across the floor of the autopsy room. Marvin's body was deposited in a bloody heap with his face torn off.

"Oh my God! Marvin?" Zach knelt and checked Marvin's pulse. He'd already bled out. Zach picked up a scalpel in case the assailant was still in the building, Then he backed over to the phone and punched in Amelia's extension.

Amelia answered. "What is it?"

"Marvin's dead. Call 911! And don't come down here."

He dropped the receiver as the doors next to the phone hissed open. A gray, naked John Doe reached for him. Zach backpedaled. Gore dangled from the corpse's slack jaw. The toe tag slid along the floor with each step. Zach was stopped at the wall. His sweaty hand gripped the scalpel. *One more step.* He plunged the scalpel into the corpse's chest. John Doe grasped Zach's bicep and pulled him close. Zach registered the stench of decay as Mr. Doe bit Zach's throat. Warm blood flowed down Zach's chest. Through the round window in the automatic door, Zach glimpsed the elevator door opening. Amelia's bulk stood there with one fat hand planted on each hip. She started toward him with purpose in her step. *I told her not to come down here. Witch versus zombie.* Zach smiled as his vision faded.

Death On The Wing

O ur small fishing boat rode gentle swells below a bloodred sky. The sea bore the squeals of bats waking from their day's rest with a voracious hunger. Stillness hung in the air like a wet blanket over this speck of an island in the South Pacific.

"Miss Jasmine?"

"Yes, Captain."

"It's getting late. Cook and Marsella are not comfortable so close to the mangrove." He gestured with a slight nod of his head.

"How about you, Captain? Are you comfortable?" Jasmine ran a hand through her short hair.

"I am paid many American dollars. Comfort will come tomorrow."

"You're right about that. What will you do with all that money?"

The captain gestured with a stub of a cigar. "I will take my family away from Mortiya. Tonga maybe? Good fishing in Tonga. Maybe a new boat. The *Pemanen Laut* is very tired."

"I've been meaning to ask you what *Pemanen Laut* means."

"Grandfather named her. It means 'the sea harvester.'"

Jasmine tilted her head at the other crewmembers. "What will Cook and Marsella do if you leave for Tonga?"

The captain smiled, revealing tobacco-stained teeth. "We fished these waters as boys. They are my family also."

Cook said something in his native tongue, pointing toward the mangrove. He was Elvis's biggest fan, but the music that usually floated around the boat was quiet that afternoon. Cook was tense, and I missed his good-natured laughter.

The captain turned to me and forced a smile. "You are sure about this?"

"I am. Are you?"

"No one has ever spent the night so close to so many devils."

"But you've lived with them all your life."

"When they reach my village, they are not so many. You can fight six or ten. Shelter is provided against a hundred. But so many?" He waved his unlit cigar in a sweeping arc. "No one knows."

"This is the last piece, Captain. Tomorrow, you'll be on your way to Tonga, and I'll be out of your hair."

"Cook will miss you."

"I will miss him as well." I gazed at the distant tangle of trees and shrubs from the bow. Mortiya was an archipelago in the South Pacific, unrenowned except for the presence of this species of bat. The mangrove we were anchored near was the only place in the world the giant vampire bat was known to nest. And the locals were determined to exterminate it. I was sent to film the creatures, which were both revered and hated by the Mortiyan people.

Cook's compact, muscled body hurried past me. He spoke in short bursts. The captain pointed to the sky. One lone speck circled above the mangrove. The sun dipped below the horizon. Twilight had arrived, and night was close behind. They say a person can smell fear. I wasn't sure what fear smelled like, but that evening, I saw it in the eyes of my friend Cook.

"Miss Jasmine, please." Marsella, the boat engineer, stood by the Plexiglas enclosure he had built for me. Three walls and a roof of plastic were screwed to the foredeck and butted against the front exterior of the cabin. A hatch was cut into the forward cabin wall for me to enter the enclosure. The added hatch infringed on the cramped space that served as both galley and dining hall.

I joined Marsella. "Is everything okay?"

He struck the enclosure with a small sledgehammer. The blow resounded in my ears. "Is good?"

"Yes, Marsella. Very strong, like you."

He smiled and turned his milky-white eye on me.

I'd traveled with these men for two weeks aboard this boat, which had seen better days. The captain, Marsella, and Cook spent much of their days fussing and nurturing her. They kept her meticulously clean. The engine, for which they could no longer find parts, was maintained through ingenuity and willpower. I learned it had been handed down through two generations. And I would bet it wasn't new when the captain's grandfather had bought it.

I'd come to know and understand the crew. They treated me with respect and indulged my wishes without complaint as we visited the chain of islands they called home. Without complaint, that is, until this last one. My wish to film the bats as they left the nest to hunt caused heated discussions and drove a wedge between us. No one wanted to spend the night in the shadow of thousands of ravenous giant vampire bats. But these dignified men were embarrassed to say so because then they would have to admit their fears.

Marsella grabbed the corners of the five-by-five-by-six-foot enclosure he'd attached to the wooden cabin. It cluttered the foredeck, leaving little room to get around it. He shook it, showing me its strength. It moved more than I'd expected—more than I'd hoped, if I was being honest. But these were bats, not bears. An adult weighed between two and three pounds. How much damage could they do in one night?

"Is okay?" he asked.

"I'll be fine. It's only one night." In spite of my confidence, I took a moment to look it over and gave it a shake of my own. "It's very good. Marsella, would you clean the top for me one last time?"

The clear roof was the most important feature of my glass box. Filming the creatures as they flew overhead in the dark would prove difficult enough. Doing it through bird shit would have been a waste of time.

He hoisted himself onto the top and used a greasy rag to wipe off the shit that had collected throughout the day.

I retreated to my equipment bag then handed him up a clean cloth and some glass cleaner. "Please. It is very important."

He shook his head but complied anyway.

I was foolish to think so, but his bad eye always seemed to hold me in contempt. During the two weeks I'd lived aboard their vessel, I should have gotten beyond such a childish reaction. I'd filmed in the most remote corners of the planet. Some were beautiful; some were cesspools. There were horrors beyond imagination in many of these places. But nothing got in the way of my work. Yet poor

Marsella's diseased eye creeped me out. And I considered myself so worldly.

A handful of dark specks circled above the mangrove now. The crew was anxious to get inside, but pride kept them on deck. They were waiting me out. Marsella jumped down from the roof.

"*Terima kasih banyak.*" I'm sure I butchered the pronunciation.

"You are most welcome, Miss Jasmine." He bowed slightly and headed off to attend to some other detail.

"Cook, let's go inside," I said. "You can play 'Blue Suede Shoes' for me."

Relief washed over his face. "The king, yes?"

I nodded and ducked into the cabin where we took our meals. That night, the crew planned to sleep in there while I filmed the bats from my glass castle. They may have referred to it as my glass casket or some variation of that. But I knew the three men didn't want any harm to come to me. They saw me as their ward, someone in their charge.

I took my customary seat on the bench and waited for dark. Elvis sang about a cold, gray Chicago morning, and layers of blue smoke mingled with the musty smell of unwashed bodies.

Marsella manicured his nails with a serious-looking knife that was ill-suited to the task. The polished eight-inch blade reflected light beams around the cabin. His good eye focused on his task, but the strange filmy eye remained trained on me.

Cook sat at the table and shuffled a deck of cards as if he were trying to wear the spots off them. An unfiltered cigarette burned as it dangled from the corner of his mouth.

Only the captain seemed relaxed, leering his brown-toothed grin in my direction. His weathered complexion matched the teak chair he leaned back in. Catching my gaze, he tilted his head back and blew a chain of smoke rings.

"So, Captain, if your country is bent on destroying these bats, why are you moving to Tonga?"

"The scientists"—he faked spitting on the floor in disgust—"have always found a way to stop it. They sent you, didn't they?"

"My job is to film the bats, not protect them. The work on the island is done. Tonight, I'll shoot the migration from the mangrove. Then you're free to kill every last one of them as far as I'm concerned."

Marsella startled me by stabbing his knife into the table. "Tonight, you see the gates of hell thrown open."

"Yes." The captain spat again. "We've planned to kill these devils many times. The scientists always cry, 'Please wait until we do this or study that.' Another year my people hide from the dark."

"Over the centuries, your people have revered the bats. Some of them *still* make sacrifices to them. Many people think it's wrong to exterminate any species of animal or plant, for that matter."

"The scientists"—he spat again—"don't have to bury the drained bodies of their children. Tonight, you film them. It will be something else tomorrow. I would bring you for nothing if I believed the devils would be destroyed."

"I understand," I said solemnly. We'd had that discussion before. For years, an international community of do-gooders managed to delay the Mortiyans' plan to rid their island of these creatures. The captain wasn't blaming me. He just needed someone to vent his frustration to. I had no skin in this game. My money was in the bank.

Elvis crooned "Love Me Tender." The atmosphere in

the cabin was anything but tender. "Don't Fear The Reaper" would have been a more appropriate soundtrack based on the tension in our crowded space.

"Have you ever thought about doing it yourself? Maybe set fire to the mangrove."

"Ha, it has been tried and failed." He lifted his chin to Marsella. "Remember '86?"

"Hard to forget that night." Marsella reached a hand to his milky eye. "The devils stole my eye."

I looked at Cook, who quickly looked away. The cabin became quiet, uncomfortably so. I was getting antsy.

The captain pointed to the roof. "It has begun." Pointing my gaze up, I remembered how the roof had leaked the day we were caught in a squall. Cook had distributed pots and pans to collect the water. I smiled at the memory of all the noise the dripping water had made as it had landed in the various containers—a cacophony of plinks and plunks.

Marsella put his knife away, rose, and motioned for me to take my position. Cook's hands faltered, spraying the cards across the rough-hewn tabletop. The hastily added hatch was opened to expose my room for the night. As I ducked into the enclosure, I glimpsed Cook kissing a crucifix he wore around his neck. Marsella closed the door, sealing me off.

I took a deep breath and stretched. Tension eased out of my muscles as soon as I lifted the camera to my shoulder. I laughed out loud, realizing how oppressive the cabin had been. The infrared motion sensors on the two tripod-mounted cameras checked out and immediately started to search for activity. I loved my high-tech gear. The technology built into my cameras would capture extraordinary photos whether I was present or not. However, the camera on my shoulder would be the one with the money shot. I'd built a reputation for capturing remarkable footage in impossible situations. That footage was what paid my bills. That night would be no exception.

The routine of checking my gear relaxed me until the image of Cook kissing his crucifix returned. The Mortiyans had blended their original beliefs with the Christianity missionaries had brought to them over two hundred years ago. They were a superstitious people by nature. The oldest residents retold legends of human sacrifices—people who were stripped and tied between two sacred trees. It was supposed to be an honor, but I would wager that no one had volunteered for that honor.

My thoughts swirled around the many conversations I'd had over the last two weeks about the devil who rained death over them nightly. Then the air was filled with a kind of high-pitched whistling that was balanced by the dull flap of leathery wings. The sound both chilled and hypnotized me simultaneously. Most of all, I was amazed by the decibels the bats could generate.

With my eye glued to the viewfinder, I fell into a rhythm as wave after wave of bats passed low over the boat. The camera softly hummed into my right ear, which was pressed against the camera body. The night sky turned into a living mass of brown, so thick at times that I couldn't see a single star in the heavens.

Finally, the migration dwindled, allowing the stars to shine through once again. My arms felt like dead weight, and my fingertips tingled from lack of circulation. Relief washed over me as I lowered the camera from my shoulder for the first time in hours. I reached for a water bottle to quench my parched throat, and started in disbelief.

The boat was covered with the creatures. They looked at me quizzically. They were hard to fear with their distinctive chocolate-brown fur highlighted by two scarlet stripes down their chests, black button eyes, and cute little rounded ears.

"I'm surrounded by teddy bears." I laughed out loud. The sound echoing off the glass walls startled me. My ears rang as if I had been attending a rock concert. The bats were quiet in small numbers, but that night I realized how much noise they made en mass. I could hear a kind of cooing sound coming from the hundreds that stared at me.

Other sounds were starting to register as well. The most annoying was an intermittent thumping as if someone was bouncing a tennis ball off the cabin wall. I dug out my still camera and started shooting portraits of the bats pressed up against the Plexiglas enclosure. Some of them jockeyed for space, but mostly they just stared. I moved around my space, shooting as many of their faces as I could. The thumping continued. At one point, I risked chasing off my subjects when I banged on the wall and yelled, "Knock it off."

My actions created a minor stir, which offered up more great shots. I banged on the glass to see what kind of response I would get. My heart stopped. One of the brackets that fastened the plastic to the ship's cabin swung loose. The screw had pulled free of the wood. One of my furry visitors gnawed at the hole left by the screw with his sharp teeth. Instinctively, I banged the glass to shoo him away. A crack appeared in the Plexiglas where Marsella had drilled the hole to attach the bracket. "Okay, okay. It's just a stress crack. Don't overreact like some helpless female. No more banging." I tried to put it out of my head and focus on the work instead.

The thumping continued. Periodically, I checked the crack. It didn't get any worse, but one bat continued to gnaw where the screw had fallen out, creating a small pile of sawdust on deck. The hole eventually grew large enough that two and sometimes three bats worried it together. Switching back to video, I filmed their relentless attack. The rest of them watched me as if they didn't understand being able to see me and not being able to get to me. It was unnerving.

There was nothing to be done about the hole they were making in the wall. I doubted they would get through, but their perseverance was impressive. I glanced around for a weapon just in case. A tripod would make an adequate club if necessary. Of course, I could always retreat into the cabin. That would put a smile on Marsella's face. Not that he meant me any ill will, but I think my self-confidence ruffled his feathers.

I poured strong black coffee into a cup from a thermos Cook had provided and snacked on my favorite local food, honey cakes. It wasn't so much a cake as it was a moist, crunchy bar with the right amount of sweetness. They were similar to the power bars consigned to the bottom of my luggage ever since Cook had first introduced me to this local treat. Reinvigorated after my break, I inspected my equipment one more time, replacing memory sticks and battery packs as necessary.

Predawn light showed on the horizon, reflecting off the perfectly calm sea. I estimated I had another hour before my subjects would take their leave.

As if on cue, some bats flew over the boat, returning home. They were sated with the blood of their victims. My camera whirred in my ear as I zoomed in to capture the images overhead. I hummed the "Teddy Bear's Picnic" song as I worked.

Finally, my fur-covered shipmates started to move around. One by one, they lifted off into the brightening sky. I filmed this last bit less than enthusiastically. My legs wobbled and sagged against the glass. I would be glad when this assignment was in my rearview mirror. With my eyes closed, I released a long, controlled breath.

The boat rocked with the incoming tide, causing me to stumble a little as I packed up my gear. I was exhausted. An early morning rum punch and a nap on deck in the sun while the captain steered us home would suit me just fine. The intermittent thump, which had stopped for a time, started up again. Stuffing a camera into a case, I noticed something wet seeping under the hatch. It was deep red, almost black in the limited light of dawn.

I banged on the door. "Is everything all right?"

I turned the latch, but the door didn't swing open. Instinctively, I reached for my camera, pressed it against my face, and hit record. I pushed my weight against the door and moved it just enough to peek into the cabin. Marsella's milky eye greeted me through the opening. It stared at me from the floor. I pushed the door against the weight of his body until I could squeeze through. The cabin was in ruins. Marsella's tattered blue overalls exposed the bites covering his body. Dozens of bats lay around him. One was still impaled on the knife clutched in his dead hand.

The captain's shredded face stared at me from behind the table he'd moved to just below where Cook dangled near a gaping hole in the roof. A bloody butcher knife lay below him next to dozens of cleaved bats. Cook had apparently been trying to close the hole in the roof over the galley. His body hung from one of the many hooks secured to the wall.

Each gentle rock of the vessel caused his dangling foot to strike the wall.

Thump.

Thump.

Thump.

Fearless

S oft clicks floated on the still air, accented by the rhythmic drip of the kitchen faucet. Jo's fingers paused above her keyboard as she reviewed the scene on her computer screen. Each drop of water massaged shards of glass into her brain. She could call the superintendent to fix it, but that would be worse. The man exacerbated her heightened senses—that was what her doctor called phobias—undermining the fragile foundation of her daily existence.

The super's tool belt jangled with every step, like a symphony orchestra endlessly tuning. Every fucking light in the apartment would get turned on, and the residual reek of garlic and cheap cigars would take a week to dissipate. Most of all, Jo hated the constant inane banter that accompanied every encounter with the super. It required three days minimum to recover from a brief visitation by him— three days she could ill afford with the publisher's deadline rushing toward her like an oncoming subway train.

She made her way through the darkened room—*drip*— to the sink—*drip*. She reached for the hand towel conveniently hung on the oven—*drip*—and draped it over the offending faucet. She blew out the breath she'd been holding in a sigh of relief and spoke to the darkness. "That's better."

A glance at the computer reminded her that Amanda, the heroine of her romantic adventure series, still lay naked on sweat-dampened sheets in the embrace of her lover. Amanda had to wait. Jo's traitorous mind took a sharp turn and accelerated toward paralyzing fear. The collapse of her psychological defenses would allow the world to flood in and wash her out to sea, where she would be tossed around in a cacophony of sound and light. She shuddered.

Her slippers scuffed softly along the carpet as she walked down the hall to the bathroom. An army of amber bottles stood at the ready. A nightlight provided enough illumination to identify the correct soldier. She shook out two pills, tossed them into her mouth, and swallowed. Panic hammered on the door, threatening to smash her fragile state. "I can't afford an episode now," she said. "Not now. Please, God! Not now."

Fatigue overtook her. The safety of her bed and a cocoon of comforters beckoned her. Unable to resist, she slipped between the sheets, pulled the covers over her head, and burrowed deep. She shivered and blew out long, slow breaths. Dread was her constant companion in those hours before sleep granted release.

Jo sat back in the comfort of a cushioned leather seat; a remote sense of movement lulled her. An abrupt stop had her sitting up, her spine rigid. Then the door opened, and she was thrust into chaos. Calliope music collided with screams. Colored lights played across people like living tattoos. She was swept along in the current of the crowd, down the midway. Amplified voices of carnies incited attendees to "step right up." The clashing aromas of popcorn, sweat, and sawdust made her stomach retch. She stumbled, landing face down in the dirt. The stampede of people trampled her. She struggled, trying to get off the ground. She pushed and kicked.

She sobbed, awakened by the dream. The blankets lay strewn on the floor where she'd shoved them away. She staggered from her bed and returned to her desk, where Amanda still lay naked in Nicholas's arms. Jo's keyboard would provide the protection her mind sought. Once immersed in her writing, she would be liberated from a life of self-bondage, fear, and shame.

Amanda left Nicholas's snores behind and climbed to the main deck of the yacht. Leaning against the bulkhead, she let the warmth of the Mediterranean breeze dry her naked skin. She was virtually alone on the water. Not another vessel was within sight in any direction. Thousands of stars reflected on the calm sea, and she didn't have to share them with anyone.

Except Jo, of course. Jo saw every sparkling gem of light in the night sky. Jo shook out her hair and welcomed the goose bumps that erupted on her body from the fresh Mediterranean breeze. The gentle rocking of the boat lulled Jo into a trance. The clicking continued as her fingers moved of their own accord across the keyboard.

The first thing Jo noticed when her eyes opened was the darkness. The computer had put itself to sleep. Reflexively, her fingers woke it from its slumber. Two words floated in the middle of the screen:

The End

Mild surprise drew her gaze down to the word count. She'd written almost thirty thousand words. In the past day, or days—she wasn't sure how many—she'd completed the novel. It was longer than usual. Eddie, her editor, would have to deal. She knew there was no need to go back and proofread. Experience told her the thirty thousand words would ring true. They would be better than anything she wrote in her conscious state. She did her best work when she traveled.

During phone interviews, she told reporters she got lost in the character. However, it was more than that, much more. When Amanda looked at the stars above the Mediterranean, Jo saw them. She heard the waves slapping against the hull of the yacht and felt the gentle rocking of the sea. When the breeze blew across Amanda's wet skin, Jo's broke out in goose flesh.

Yes, she experienced her characters' lives in the flesh. If she stepped into the story, the question that begged asking was, who remained behind? Who typed in her absence? She couldn't follow that train of thought for long, or she would require a Xanax breakfast with a side of Ativan and a glass of Bombay Sapphire gin.

She pushed those thoughts away and busied herself with formatting the manuscript before emailing it to her agent and publisher a full two weeks ahead of the deadline.

Emails sailed into the ether with the familiar whoosh. Only then did she push her stiff skeletal frame out of the chair. Her joints cracked and popped with resentment at the abuse she'd leveled on them. There was no doubt Jo's body had been in the chair, typing, for God knew how many hours while she'd accompanied Amanda island-hopping in the Mediterranean, searching for her missing friend and juggling lovers.

Under the hot water that softly fell from the rain shower-head, she thought about the days ahead. Eventually, she would read the prose written in her absence. For the time being, she would wait for her editors to read it and respond. Their suggestions and corrections had proven to be invaluable, but very few of those edits had involved the sections written while she'd… traveled. The sections that materialized when she escaped from her self-made prison were usually flawless. Most often, the transitions between her conscious writing and what she'd written while she traveled needed smoothing out. She smiled into the steamed-up mirror at the thought of traveling. Then she wrapped a towel around her body and dried her short hair with another.

She got around pretty well for a woman who only left her apartment once every six months to appease her psychiatrist. All her banking was done electronically, online shopping fulfilled her modest needs, she cut her own hair, and her groceries were delivered from the local market. This last thought made her smile.

The young woman who had been delivering her food for the past year was a fan. On her first visit, she had tried to get Jo to open the door. Standing in the hall, talking to the closed door, she explained that someone might take Jo's delivery. Finally, she admitted she was a fan. Then she produced Jo's most recent novel, a hardback copy of *Cali-*

fornia Gold, and held it up to the peephole. Hardback sales represented a small portion of the books Jo sold. Her fans mostly used e-readers. Paperback sales were a close second.

"I-I… could you, I mean, I hoped you would auto-graph it for me. My name is Amanda too."

Jo scribbled a note and slid it under the door. *Leave it. Come back tomorrow.*

The girl tilted her freckled face after reading the note and peered at the peephole. "But…"

Then she reverently set the book next to the groceries and turned away. She disappeared from Jo's limited field of view, but the chime on the elevator did not ding for several minutes. Jo waited, her face pressed against the peephole. When the bell finally announced the arrival of the elevator car, she opened the door and pulled the bag inside. She was annoyed by the intrusion of the girl but signed the book anyway.

To Amanda with Freckles,
May your travels be as interesting and varied as our heroine's.
Jo Scott

She hung the canvas shopping bag on the door with the book inside. The next day, a note appeared under her door.

I'm sorry to have bothered you. Thank you for signing my book. Please don't tell the manager. I need this job. I will not bother you again. Promise.
Amanda with Freckles

Jo smiled at the girl's adoption of the moniker. She had planned to tell the grocer not to send the girl again, but the next time she emailed her order, she didn't mention it.

True to her word, Amanda with Freckles never both-ered her again, although she continued to deliver Jo's groceries. Every week, Jo received a note, a simple "hi" accompanied by some random thought. Sometimes it was a quote from one of Jo's novels or something about empowering women, but most often, the girl just wrote simple well wishes. "I hope you're doing well," or "I can't wait for your next novel." She always signed with a freckled smiley face.

Jo collected the notes in a neat pile on her otherwise austere desk. Eventually, she started leaving notes pinned to the empty canvas bag for Amanda. Jo asked about her interests, what she did when she wasn't at work, and whether she had a boyfriend. Six months into their anony- mous correspondence, the notes became longer. Jo learned that Amanda hoped to be a writer someday. Theatre, creative writing, and literature were her favorite classes. Math and science were hard, but she managed good grades in those too.

Jo's weekly correspondence with Amanda was the closest thing to a personal relationship she'd had in years, since college really. It was mostly one-way. She shared very little about herself. But she looked forward to their weekly chats. She often wondered how much Amanda knew about her, aside from the press releases her publicist put out. Jo knew that persistent researchers had ways of finding things out no matter how well-hidden they were. Her pre-Jo Scott incarnation lurked out there somewhere.

Back at her desk, Jo saw two messages in her inbox. The first was from The Justin Cooke Agency.

Jo,

Great job, Hun. Eddie is already poring over the manuscript and smiling like the carnival clown in the dunk tank. It's a little longer than usual, but we'll squeeze it between the covers.

Thanks Doll,

Justin

The other email was from Eddie.Banks@hachettebook-group.com

Jo,

I love it so far. Two things to think on: Did you have a title in mind? Have you given any thought to punching up the sex scenes? They are becoming a little predictable.

Eddie

Eddie had suggested that she "punch up" the sex before. Last time, he had specifically asked her to make the sex scene rougher. She'd ignored that little tidbit. She should send Eddie something to get him off her case. Maybe she could describe what rough sex was really like to Eddie as well as the aftermath. The unending parade of hospitals, detectives, doctors, and drugs. The relentless fear. She could tell him about her prison seventy-six floors above the most exciting city in the world that was one short cab ride from 118th Street near Lenox.

No, she couldn't write that. She adored Eddie for his invaluable suggestions regarding her work. He had been especially helpful in the early days with her first couple of novels. She would never forget the gentle nurturing and encouragement he'd provided. He had gently schooled her without judgment to become the writer she was today.

There was plenty of time to consider the title. For the moment, she would take it easy. With her deadline met and nothing to do, she took two Seroquel and went to bed.

Before sleep fogged her busy mind, her thoughts drifted back to Amanda with Freckles. *What do you think, Amanda? Do you have any title ideas?*

Amanda's imagined voice echoed in Jo's head. "How about Mediterranean Blue?"

I love it. I'll emphasize her sadness in the blurb to hit on the double meaning behind blue. That's perfect.

Jo awoke feeling groggy. She hated taking Seroquel for

that reason, which was the same reason she didn't like the other medications in her bathroom cabinet and didn't take them as prescribed. They interfered with her work. She would take a day off before tackling her new idea. She had outlined a paranormal romance series. The details of the world still needed to be nailed down. Once that was complete, she planned to immerse herself in that world for a couple months and see what emerged. She had time before she needed to return to the Amanda Grant series.

She started the coffee maker and woke up her computer. She saw an email from the doorman: "I delivered a heavy box. Alex" This was equivalent to holding out his hand. A tip was expected whenever Alex did something for a resident. She would handle that later. A heavy box meant only one thing—the prerelease of her latest novel. This would be the finished product unless she spotted a glaring mistake, which never happened.

She pulled the box inside the door and slid it to her desk. After she finally got the carton open, she extracted a hardback edition of *Arctic White, an Amanda Grant Novel*. She examined the cover, spine, and back, then the inside flaps. She moved to a comfortable chair then started reading, only pausing to refresh her coffee. When she finally closed the book, she sent a message to Eddie, her editor, and cc'd Justin, her agent.

Eddie,

Arctic White is good to go. The cover looks beautiful. Thanks for all your hard work and attention to detail.

Jo

Jo placed an advance copy of *Arctic White* in a canvas shopping bag a month before the official release. She hung it on the door and waited for Amanda the True to arrive with her order from the market. Jo heard the door handle rattle and rushed to watch. Amanda set the order on the

floor and retrieved the usually empty bag waiting for her.
She peered inside at the unexpected weight. Amanda's eyes
lit up when she opened the book to the title page.

To Amanda the True,
    You are true to your word. Thanks for the smiles.
    Yours,
    Jo Scott :~)

Amanda pulled her note from the bag of groceries,
added something to it, and returned it to the bag.

Jo waited until she was gone. She carried the groceries
into the kitchen and extracted the note.

*I'm sorry I won't be your delivery person anymore. I've been
accepted to Columbia. Good luck. Never stop writing. You can't know
how much joy your books bring the world. Thank you for being my
friend this past year. I'll never forget it.*

After the freckled smiley face, she'd added,

*Thank you for the book. I can't wait to get started on it. You're an
inspiration.*

    Your Friend,
    Amanda the True

Jo was shocked. She'd known Amanda the True was
applying to colleges, but the suddenness of her departure
threw Jo. She had a million questions for Amanda the
True. Did she know that Jo had graduated from Columbia
with a degree in English Literature or that she'd returned
after graduation to continue her studies in pursuit of a
career as an instructor, maybe even a professor? No, probably not. That was another life, a more carefree time, and
a different person. That was before a person named Jo
Scott existed.

Back then, her idiosyncrasies were considered quirky.
That was before the parade of psychiatrists, those men and

women with their degrees and prescription pads who wanted to help her. How could they possibly help when they had never been held down on a dirty mattress in an abandoned building off 118ᵗʰ Street near Lenox Avenue? They hadn't been stripped naked, savagely beaten, and left for dead in the freezing cold. How could they help? She couldn't help herself, except when she wrote.

She should have warned Amanda the True of the impending danger. Jo's fear meter started redlining again. Could she warn Amanda the True? What would she say? "Don't ride the subway at night. Stay away from abandoned buildings." No, none of those things could keep Amanda the True safe. The girl would need to build her own prison to keep the world out. It was the only way to be safe. Could Jo tell her that? *No.* Would Amanda the True believe her? *Probably not.* Who could understand? *No one, unless I tell them why, and I won't do that. Can't do that.* Instead, she had changed her name, escaped into anonymity, and wrote novels in seclusion.

She shuffled toward the bathroom. Her hip brushed against the layers of heavy drapes over the window. The slight movement allowed the noise from the Hudson River to leak inside her apartment for an instant. It served as a reminder of the tenuous barrier between the outside world and her solitary confinement. The blaring horns and flashing lights of the river pushed against her flimsy defenses endlessly, just as it harassed the levies keeping it within its banks, day after day, without rest. Thinking about it exhausted her.

Her hands shook as she reached for a medicine bottle. She spiraled toward a panic attack. It was Amanda's fault. Jo crawled into bed, praying for dream-free sleep to take her quickly. Her prayer went unanswered.

Jo stood in the dark, quite alone. A circle of light beckoned to her. Like a moth, she was unable to resist its attraction. She stepped forward, her heels clicking on the hardwood beneath her feet. Pandemonium erupted when she entered the circle. The house lights were brought up, and she faced an auditorium of smiling people.

Amanda the True stood in the front row, naked and bleeding. The crowd applauded and chanted Jo's name. They all wanted her, wanted a piece of her. There was not enough of her to go around. They surged forward. Amanda the True disappeared amidst the chaos. Jo ran to her but found herself immersed in a sea of grasping hands and shouting voices. They carried her along in their jubilance and demanded her attention.

She called out to Amanda the True, but there was no response. She'd vanished under the grinding heels. When Jo reached the last place she'd seen Amanda the True, all she found was a stack of notes with freckled smiley faces on them.

Jo woke at her glass-and-chrome desk, clutching the notes Amanda had written to her over the last year. The weak light that bled around the heavy drapes provided just enough illumination to see that much. The nightmare was fading, but the image of Amanda standing naked with her flesh battered and bleeding persisted. "How did I get here? Did I walk in my sleep last night? That's a first." She remembered taking something and going to bed. That usually kept the dreams away. She stood up and felt sore muscles she didn't know she had. She certainly had not used them.

In the kitchen, she put on the coffee. Every bend and stretch made her ache. "What the hell did I do last night?"

She sat at her desk and woke her iMac. A new document appeared on the screen.

The wind swirled through the urban canyon, blowing the discarded detritus of an absentee culture down an empty street. Leaning against an abandoned building, I kept vigil near the subway entrance. A sniper would recognize my stillness and patience as the hallmarks of training and discipline. For me, they were merely tools, a means to an end. I waited. Footfalls clicked on the cold concrete. A young woman labored under the weight of a backpack. I tensed and kept to the shadows, following along. The young woman passed through a circle of light.

A dark figure on the other side of the street stealthily closed in on her. I mirrored his movement. A chemical odor wafted to me as he closed the distance between himself and the young woman. I made my move as he extended a hand clutching a rag toward his intended victim. The crackling sound of my Taser halted his motion and sent him convulsing to the broken sidewalk. His crotch darkened when his bladder let go.

"Run!" I pointed at the girl. "Go. Now!" Her trainers slapped the cold pavement, and the backpack bounced up and down toward the subway station.

With the chloroform-soaked rag safely stuffed into my pocket, I zapped the stranger again. Why did he have to be so big? This presented a challenge, but I managed to drag him into the abandoned building, where we wouldn't be disturbed. The hours I'd practiced tying knots ensured he stayed put. Patiently and methodically, I applied a tourniquet at the base of his genitals. Unblinking, I detached them from his groin. My kitchen shears were ill-suited to the task, and I made a mess of the job. *Note to self; use a sharp knife next time.*

The wind howled through the empty building. The hunter-turned-prey started to come around, pain and fear clearing his mind of the fog. The shock of his missing body components replaced the electrical shock he'd received earlier. He watched as I cut his penis into bite-size bits. I poised my shears above his eye. "You can be blind and dickless or just dickless. It's up to you."

"No. Please, no more. I'll do anything," he whimpered.

At that, I fed him his own cock, one piece at a time.

Jo was horrified by the graphic nature of what she'd written. Her finger reached for the delete button and paused. Her hand trembled above the keyboard, unable to complete the task. Instead, she pushed away from the desk and headed for the bathroom. At the medicine cabinet, she waited to see which of her fears would raise the alarm. To her surprise, nothing rushed in to threaten her. The normal debilitating anxiety that constituted her everyday life lay dormant.

Instead, confusion reigned. For lack of a better idea, she took a long shower. Hot water filled her bathroom with steam. The simple pleasure filled her with contentment. Her mind wanted to remember when she had gotten out of bed to write, but the sense of well-being repeatedly pushed it aside. She felt around for a towel and her robe. The thick mist obscured the little night-light. A groan from her stomach prompted her to go to the kitchen, still dripping, to get something to eat.

For the first time in years, she prepared a proper breakfast, including two eggs, bacon, and a toasted garlic bagel, which to her amazement, she finished. She carried a second cup of coffee into the dining room and reread the —she didn't know what to call it. Was it a story, an essay, or what? As she read, she watched the scene play out in her mind, recalling details not expounded upon on the page, like the fear in the young woman's eyes when she turned to see her would-be assailant or the gagging noise made by her victim when she force-fed him. These elements were easily recognized yet difficult to put into words.

"This is crazy, even for me." She snugged the belt of her robe and went to get the morning paper from the hall. When she turned to the metro section, she froze. A black-and-white photo of Amanda the True stared from the page.

VIGILANTISM ALIVE AND WELL

An unknown woman spared Amanda Evers from a mugging last night at approximately 10:00 p.m. in the area of Lenox Avenue and 118th Street. Ms. Evers was unable to provide the police with any further information. "It all happened so fast. I turned to see this man reaching for me. Then I heard that zappy thing, and a woman's voice shouted for me to run. When I reached the subway platform, I called 911." A search of the area turned up one Raymond C. Herring, hog-tied in an adjacent building. His penis and testicles had been severed. A spokesman for the NYPD stated that Mr. Herring had suffered from blood loss and exposure. Mr. Herring is a convicted sex offender who has been in and out of the system for years.

Jo stopped reading, feeling light-headed and a little giddy.

The Guardian

"I will have that book!"

From the back room, Syd heard the anger in the customer's voice. She moved to the doorway to eavesdrop.

"Set your price!"

"It's not for sale." Scott's voice barely carried through the displays of books and dusty shelves. At ninety-one, nothing Scott did went far or fast.

"This is a bookstore, isn't it?"

"I don't know what you read in that book, sir, but I assure you, it's not for sale, not at any price."

"Have it your way." The floor shook with a crash.

Syd's mind jumped to dreadful scenarios as she bolted toward the source of the noise.

"I'm not leaving without it." The customer's voice had lost its anger and sounded strained.

"Syd!" Scott called.

Making her way around the last of the tall shelves, Syd saw the customer clutch his left arm and crumple to the floor. Ignoring him, she turned to Scott. "Are you all right?"

Scott leaned on his walking stick amidst scattered books and an overturned cart. "Yes, I'm fine. See to him." He gestured to the customer with his phone. "Yes, operator, I'm here."

Syd felt for a pulse. Finding none, she reviewed what little she knew about CPR. *Clear the airway. Tilt the head back.* Her resource was suspect; learning to save someone's life on a television sitcom was not ideal, but it was all she had to go on. *I'm glad Arizona has a Good Samaritan law. What was that stupid disco song they said had the right rhythm? Oh yeah, The Bee Gees. Ugh.* She began chest compressions.

"One moment." Scott pressed the phone to his chest. "Syd, do you know CPR?" He got back on the phone. "Yes, operator, my assistant apparently knows CPR. She's either trying to save him or strangle him. Hard to say from my position."

The warmth of the Arizona afternoon had seeped into the store. The temperature combined with the effort she was exerting made sweat form on her brow. Keeping someone's heart pumping was demanding. *It looks so easy on television.*

"I agree, operator, it's not a joking matter, but if you knew my assistant, you'd understand my ambivalence."

Sirens drowned out Scott's banter with the 911 operator, and Syd renewed her efforts. Within minutes, the bell over the door announced the arrival of the Scottsdale Fire Department. Four men wearing traditional blue shorts and snug T-shirts hovered over Syd. The first knelt across from her and nodded. "Count out loud for me."

Syd rolled her eyes and sang, "Staying alive, staying alive, uh uh uh uh, staying alive."

"Don't quit your day job." The EMT smiled and took over.

She pushed back on her heels. Sweat trickled from her

brow and burned her eyes. She rubbed them with the back of her hand to clear her vision.

Scott dropped into his desk chair and motioned her over. "Ignore them and sit." He pulled a bottle of Johnny Walker Black and two mason jars from an ancient oak desk, poured liberally, and handed one to Syd.

The jar shook in her sweaty grip. She threw the whiskey back then banged the empty jar down on his desk. "Don't you ever do that to me again." Her voice quavered.

"What did *I* do?"

Her trembling hand pointed to the books all over the floor. "I thought *you* hit the floor."

"Yes, but—"

"But nothing. I thought you fell. God knows you won't use your walker."

"Just so I'm understanding you correctly, you're angry at me because I'm *not* hurt?"

"Don't pull that logical bullshit on me when I'm mad." She swiped her hand through her short hair. "Besides, who's cleaning up that mess?"

Scott waggled his eyebrows. "With my knees as they are, I guess…"

She pointed a thumb at her chest. "Me. That's who."

He flashed his most charming smile.

"Wipe that smirk off your face. I should leave it. Customers can search for titles on their hands and knees."

A firefighter cleared his throat. "Excuse the interruption, but I have a few questions." He tapped a pen on his clipboard.

"How can I help you, young man?" Scott asked.

"Who called it in?"

"I did." Scott handed over a business card with a flourish. "I'm the proprietor."

"Do you know the patient?"

"Is he…" Syd hesitated.

"I can only tell you he's on his way to Osborn Medical Center."

"No," Scott continued. "He walked in about a half hour ago, browsed a while, and then…"

The fireman turned to Syd. His appraising gaze took a stroll along her figure. "And you are?"

Scott presented another business card. "My assistant, Sydney Steinert."

He added Syd's card to his clipboard. "Where did you learn to do chest compressions?"

"Why?" This time it was Syd who did the appraising. "Did I do it right?"

"You probably saved his life." His smile was perfection even if it was a little bit automatic. "So where did you learn your technique?"

Her neck and face blossomed with heat. *"The Office."*

"You were trained here?" He looked at Scott. "I wish more shopkeepers would train their employees for medical emergencies."

"Not here. *The Office* on TV. You know, with Steve Carell. I watch the reruns."

He erupted with laughter. "And they say there's nothing good on television." This time, his smile reached his eyes.

"Cap," a younger firefighter yelled. "The patient's en route, and we're cleaned up." Then he flipped open *that fucking book*.

"Be careful with that volume, please," Scott said. "It's irreplaceable."

"Hey, Cap. Look here," the firefighter said.

"Don't touch, Gopher," Cap warned.

"Here we go again," Scott muttered as he touched Syd's knee and tilted his head.

"I got it." She stood and joined the young firefighter.

"I-I just flipped it open and…" He gestured to the open book. "I'm getting married in a couple of weeks, you see, and my fiancée wants us to write our own vows. Can I copy this?"

Syd saw only a blank page. "You know that copying isn't the same as writing your own, right?"

"Oh yeah, I know, but we haven't been able to come up with much. I think she'll like this, and we can personalize it. Do you mind if I copy it?"

"No photos." She pointed to a small sign and retrieved a legal pad and pen for him from the desk. "Here you go. Close the book when you've finished."

"Yeah, sure, and thanks." He bent to the task, and the pen began scratching away.

She went back to Scott's desk and poured more Johnny Walker into her glass.

"Are we through here?" Scott asked.

"Just one more question for the young lady," the captain said.

Syd sipped her drink and waited.

Cap nodded at her tattoos. "You've got some really great ink."

"Each one has a story to tell," Scott interjected. "Or so I've been led to believe."

"Ignore him." She waved a hand at Scott. "Is there a question in there? One I missed?"

"Can I call you? For a drink or something?" His handsome features colored a little. "And a story maybe."

"Number's on the card." She pointed to his clipboard. "Office and cell."

He glanced down at the card then back at her. "You're sure? This is a little irregular."

"You're not planning a new career as a serial killer, are you, Cap?"

"Not today." He gave her his own card. "Please, call me Ken."

She bit back a comment about him two-timing Barbie, but a smirk blossomed on her face as she considered the anatomical features of Barbie's Ken. She suppressed that as well and extended her hand. "It's a pleasure, Captain Ken."

"Just Ken. I'll be in touch." He clicked his pen. "Come on, Gopher, let's get back to the house."

"Coming, Cap." The soon-to-be-married Gopher brought the pen and pad back and handed it to Scott. "Thanks a lot."

When the door closed, Syd glanced around the store to make sure they were alone. "*That fucking book* again. What's it going to take before you get rid of it? Or at least put it away somewhere. It might have killed that guy."

"I believe it's done far worse than give one contemptible would-be book thief a heart attack." He poured himself a second drink. "One day soon, we'll have that talk about *The Harbinger*, or *that fucking book*, as you so gleefully refer to it."

"Oooh, sarcasm. I'm rubbing off on you."

"It was only a matter of time before your malevolent influence had an adverse effect on my pure moral principles." Scott grinned at her. "I'm surprised I lasted two years."

"Has it been two years?" She'd wandered into Alcuin Books to absorb the air-conditioning after futilely beating the bricks, looking for temporary work. She was hot, tired, and broke. She chose a bookstore because loitering was against the law, but no one ever stopped a person from hanging out in a bookstore. They called it browsing. Because of her questionable legal status, she was careful not to fall into the clutches of the system. She couldn't know if any of her past infractions would catch up to her. More problematic were her credentials. They'd been created out of thin air by a broker whose own bona fides were suspect. She hadn't known if they would hold up under scrutiny.

"Next week in fact." Scott chuckled. "I remember how angry you were that first day."

"All I wanted was a chair, a book, and some air-conditioning. Instead, I got a heated debate over the role of religion and government in society."

"It was like a morgue in here as I recall." Scott took a small sip of his whiskey. "I needed a little excitement to liven the place up."

Syd grabbed a cold water out of the mini fridge under the counter. "We livened it up but good. I'm surprised no one called the cops."

"You did get rather boisterous."

"You baited me." Syd pointed an accusing finger at Scott. "Then you pulled books off *your* shelves to support *your* argument."

Scott chuckled, which led to a coughing fit. When he caught his breath, he continued. "Home court, as they say. Shall we do it again next week to commemorate your anniversary? Perhaps invite the local constabulary?"

"I don't think so. I don't have time to research data for my rebuttal. I still have to clean up this mess and prepare the books in back to be shipped." Syd righted the cart then moved to the books scattered on the floor. "Besides, if you make me that furious again, I'm liable to pop you a good one."

"Before we launch into the art of pugilism, I'm going

home for a nap." He set his glass on his desk. "I probably shouldn't finish this."

"Don't be surprised if *that*"—she pointed to the object of their earlier discussion—"mysteriously disappears in your absence."

He paused at the door and gave her that look, the one that reduced her to a little girl being scolded by an indulgent parent. *Not that my mother ever scolded me. It would have interfered with her getting high or laid.*

"We *will* have that talk soon," Scott said. Then the bell over the door rang as he let himself out.

Two years already. This is the longest I've stayed in one place since I split. She'd left home at thirteen and had never looked back. She drained the bourbon from Scott's glass and allowed it to warm her throat. Once she got all the books off the floor and archived, she pushed the cart to the front, past the lectern where *that fucking book* was perched.

She gazed at the hand-tooled burgundy leather cover. Flipping it open, she exposed the beautiful silk used to line the inside of the cover. They revealed only part of the story. The hand-stitched binding and the gilded-edged pages led one to believe the book was a volume of great wisdom. The workmanship was comparable to the hand-crafted books copied by monks prior to the invention of the printing press.

However, that was where it fell short. The pages were blank. Every last one. Syd had leafed through it with delicate care the first time Scott had left her alone to mind the store. The book had not so much as a blemish from cover to cover unless, according to Scott, it had something to say to the person looking at it. Then and only then would words appear, and only to the person meant to read them. She flipped through the first few pages. They remained unmarred under her gaze. "Damn it."

Her boots shook the shelves as she strode to the back. The busy work of packing books to be shipped freed her mind to consider what she was still doing there two years later. *I vowed never to fall prey to the miserable wretches that inhabit the planet. For nine years, I kept my promise to trust no one, let no one in. Keep moving. A rolling stone gathers no moss. Scott would know the origin of that gem. What the hell happened? Scott Hendrickson— that's what happened. In a couple of hours on a brain-scorching summer day, one old man accomplished what no one else has in nine years. He disarmed me. He snuck in under my radar and wore down my shields.*

She moved with swift efficiency, packing and labeling boxes. Each one received rougher handling until the banging brought a shower of dust upon her head. She looked up in disgust. *My Harley's collecting dust when she should be spreading her wings. Maybe I should blow this Popsicle stand.*

Syd carried the packages to the front as Scott shuffled through the door, looking rested.

"Been busy, I see." He took his seat at his desk and woke the computer.

Syd glanced over his shoulder as he typed in the password for the website. She had made fun of his antiquated accounting system that first day. Seeing an opportunity, she'd offered to bring Alcuin Books into the twenty-first century. Syd had created an inventory and bookkeeping system, as well as a website to promote online sales.

The gleaming iMac on his desk and the iPad she was currently using had replaced his old calculator and ledger book. She'd learned on the fly, utilizing the expertise of the staff at the Apple Store. *I was going to leave as soon as I finished that project. Take the money and run, as the song goes.*

Scott cleared his throat. "I say, you've been busy."

"You know me, ever the industrious employee." She pulled a musty-smelling box from under the front counter.

It was one of twelve that Scott had brought back from a recent estate sale. She sorted and catalogued the books into the iPad.

"Sydney, can you explain how this PayPal thing works again? I fear I will wake up one day to an empty establishment and no money in the bank."

"Trust me." She reached over his shoulder, punched in the Alcuin Books vendor number, and hit accept. "As long as my check is issued from that account, I won't let it run dry."

"That's very reassuring of you. Thank you so much."

"You know I'm here for you. If you relied solely on the people who come through the door, we would both be living on the street."

"I won't deny it. However, let's not forget I wasn't destitute yet when we met."

"Yet being the operative word there." She returned to cataloguing, when she heard Scott's chair squeak. She looked up to see him watching her. "Do you need something else?"

"We should do something special next week. A celebration for two years of continuous acrimony."

"If that means putting up with a stubborn, cantankerous old man who is stuck in his old ways, then I'm all in."

He laughed. "I believe that is the Oxford Dictionary definition verbatim."

Syd pulled the second box out and started on it. "Are we thinking a cupcake from Sprinkles or dinner at Lon's?"

"That's a very broad range. I guess the unaimed arrow never misses. Set that box aside for a minute and talk to me."

"Believe it or not, I can actually dust old books and talk

too." She stopped and slid into her chair. "You have my complete and undivided attention."

"Better." He scooted his chair over to be closer to her. "Lon's, that's at the Hermosa Inn?"

"That's the rumor. I've never been."

"Would you like that? We'll need a reservation."

"Or a sub from Tony's. No reservations needed there."

"Get back to work." He waved a dismissing hand, turned his chair around, and mumbled, "A day-old cupcake from Sprinkles is more than you deserve."

"Well, if we're going to talk about what I deserve, then we need to raise the bar substantially."

Scott pecked away at his keyboard in silence as she worked through the new acquisitions. When she slid the last carton out, she noticed the lack of retina-searing light coming through the front window. *It must be near closing.* Her nose itched, and she felt grimy from handling this particular collection of books. She was thinking about the hot shower that awaited her upstairs. The apartment above the store had been Scott's residence until he'd become unable to navigate the stairs. He had moved to a small ranch home and left the rooms upstairs furnished and vacant. Syd had taken occupancy shortly after she'd started working for Scott.

He had offered her the apartment the same day he'd had her fill out some paperwork that included the address of the dump she had been renting. She'd suspected he knew of the rundown motel and its less than sterling reputation. He had made her an offer she couldn't refuse later that day. She'd quarreled with him about the inadequate rent he had asked for, but she couldn't argue with his logic. Anything was better than nothing, and nothing was exactly what he had been collecting.

"Lights out, kid. I'll see you in the morning." Scott ambled to the front door.

"I'm going to finish this last box before I head up. Good night."

He shook his head and grinned as he switched off the open sign.

"If you have something to say…" She waited.

He rattled his key ring. "I'm taking the fifth." He closed and locked the door.

The next morning over coffee, Sydney called Captain Ken.

"Ken Stanley."

"Hey, Ken. It's Syd from Alcuin Books."

"Good morning, Syd. I was—"

She interrupted. "Ken, I'm calling to check on the guy you carried out of here yesterday. How is he doing?"

"I don't honestly know. We prick 'em and ship 'em. It's up to the docs after that."

"Charming. Do you have his name at least?"

"I don't think his name will help you. Privacy policies being what they are these days, I don't think they'll tell you anything. I'm not sure I'm at liberty to share his name even."

"I just wanted to see how he was, maybe take him some flowers."

"I have no reason to think he won't recover. Osborn does good work. Sorry I can't be more help."

"Yeah, me too." *If only he had purchased something, but of course he didn't. I need to know what that book said to him.*

"Hey, while I have you on the horn, I'm off duty next Tuesday. It's the start of my three days off. Do you to want grab a burger or something?"

"I could do that. Tuesday, we close at six. I could meet you. Say seven."

"Do you know Rehab Burger on Second Street?" he asked.

"Sure. Until next Tuesday, then."

"In the meantime, I'll see if I can get any info on your customer."

"That would be nice. Thank you." Syd disconnected.

She reviewed the overnight Twitter exploits of the president before heading downstairs while steadying a full cup of coffee with the iPad under her arm. The bell over the door sounded, drawing her to the front of the store. Scott shuffled to his desk. "You're in early," she said.

"Big day." He pointed his cane at her. "There's an online auction. You're going to do the valuation and bid up our competitors."

She sipped her coffee. "What are you going to do while I'm doing all the work?"

"I may put my feet up and take a nap. Why do you ask?"

"Only because I want to make sure you're pulling your weight. I don't know how you can sleep when *your* president has us on the brink of nuclear war anyway."

"He's your president too, and one of the many wisdoms I have acquired over the years is the importance of a good nap. It puts the Armageddon question in perspective. The preview starts in a few minutes, so scoot yourself over here."

They sat shoulder to shoulder, reviewing books. The sale was a large, diverse collection from current genre fiction to historical, including some very desirable one-of-a-kind volumes. Scott clicked through the items on his desktop, and Syd researched the provenance of the more promising offerings on her iPad. In short order, they had a list that Syd would work from during the auction.

Scott left her and puttered around the store, shelving the books she'd cleaned, catalogued, and priced the night before. *This is how two years slips through your fingers, one peaceful moment at a time. I really should get my shit together and get out of this town.*

Once the auction got under way, Syd felt the adrenaline flowing through her system. The bidding invigorated her, and more time slipped by without notice. They were down to the last few lots, and she'd done pretty well so far. She decided to pursue lot number 479. Her guilty pleasure was horror, and that particular collection contained some of everything. The complete first edition catalogue by America's premier horror writer, Stephen King, would make a nice display in the store, even though all his books were still in print. Also well-represented were Neil Gaiman, Joe Hill, and Peter Straub, to name a few. Of particular interest to Syd were several books by M.R. James, published in the early nineteenth century. Her opinion was that James had single-handedly saved the ghost story genre from choking on its own clichés. These and a few volumes like them would make bidding this lot tricky.

She took a few deep breaths to slow her heart rate and focused. Twenty minutes later, Syd was rewarded with the winning bid. Now she would have to justify the expenditure to Scott. She wasn't too worried, but it was his money after all, and they had not previously discussed that lot in particular. *It's more expedient to beg for forgiveness than to ask for permission.* She was convinced she would recover the cost of the lot by reselling the more pedestrian items quickly. That would give her the breathing space she would need to market the bigger-ticket items. Of course, she hoped to claim the M.R. James collection as her own.

A couple days later, the back room overflowed with cases of books—the fruits of her first auction. She opened cartons and examined the contents, checking them against the packing slips. The cataloguing would take weeks. She decided to tackle it the same way she would eat an elephant, one bite at a time, or in this instance, one book at a time. She photographed, wrote descriptions, priced them, and listed them on the website. If she were lucky, many of them would be sold before she had to find room for them on the shelves in the store.

Scott was in Globe to examine what remained of an old public library. He was convinced nothing would come of it, but he'd gone anyway. She was immersed in adding files to the website, when a customer came in. She jumped to her feet and met him near the door.

The heart attack victim from the other day stared at her uncertainly. "I was told a young lady saved my life in here last week. Are you her?" His lip sneered a little at the question.

In spite of what she thought of this jackass, she tried to be polite. "Guilty as charged. Can I help you with something?"

"I guess I owe you a thank you."

"Don't be silly. It was nothing."

"Is the owner here?" He started to walk around her. "I was in the middle of a negotiation with him when…"

She sidestepped and stayed in front of him. "I'm sorry. He stepped out. How can I help you?" Her hand slid into the pocket of her jeans, where it found the box cutter she'd been using that morning.

"You can wrap that book for me." He leaned around her and pointed to *that fucking book*.

"I'm sorry, but I didn't catch your name."

"I didn't give my name. I'll pay cash." Again, he tried to move around her.

She held her ground. "I believe you know that book isn't for sale. But do you mind telling me why it means so much to you?" Her hand wrapped around the box cutter, and she tensed.

"I do mind. Now if you'll fetch my purchase and tell me how much, I'll be on my way."

Her patience was wearing thin. *Hold it together.* "Again, that book is not for sale. Now I'm going to have to ask you to leave." A line her mother had often said to her when she was a kid flashed through her mind. "*I brought you into this world, and I can damn sure take you out.*" She would have to paraphrase it to fit this situation.

The man raised his arm to move her aside. Once he made contact, she was through being polite. The box cutter was out before she thought about it. "Look here, asshole. I saved your life; don't make me regret it." The little razor-sharp blade reflected a beam of light across his face. "Now back off."

He backed toward the door. "This isn't over. Not by a long shot." He threw open the door and stormed out.

"I guess it's true what they say. No good deed goes unpunished." All morning, Sydney flipped the Be Right Back sign around and locked the door whenever she left the front unattended. It was a pain in the ass, but she wouldn't risk that jackass sneaking in and snatching the book on her watch. She didn't understand Scott's reason, but he insisted the book remain on display. The bell sounded, and two women stepped inside and removed their sunglasses. Syd waited while their eyes adjusted to the comparative darkness.

The blonde smiled at her companion. She'd obviously

had some work done but not too much. "You'll be here, I assume."

"Have fun shopping, dear." The brunette kissed her partner on the cheek. "Remember, we're about out of space for shoes."

"And books," the blonde called before she headed out and closed the door behind her.

"Can I help you find anything?" Syd asked.

The brunette looked fifty-something, but Syd guessed she was actually in her sixties. She was well-preserved and smelled of old money. "Nothing specific. I'm mostly interested in biographies and historical nonfiction."

"If you prefer to browse, take all the time you like. We have a vast collection of Napoleon's writings back there." Syd gestured with a dust cloth. "Some have been translated, but many are in French. Early American presidents are on your left. Religious writings are back there on the right."

The customer held up her hand. "I get the picture."

Syd resumed her work, answering questions when asked. Eventually, she found herself showing the woman the new arrivals she'd unboxed that morning. A pile of books steadily grew on the front counter.

Sometime later, the blonde returned, schlepping elegantly wrapped bundles from the local boutiques. Her gaze fell on the pyramid of books piled on the counter, and the women laughed at one another.

Scott walked in behind the blonde, looking exhausted and a little confused. "Good afternoon, ladies. Have I missed a well-told joke?"

Syd tossed the dust cloth at him. "You missed all the excitement."

"You must be the owner of this delightful emporium," the brunette said. "Janet." She reached out her left hand, allowing Scott to keep his right hand on the walking stick.

"It is my oasis in an otherwise literary desert." Scott bowed his head. "Are these all for you?"

"I don't think she's done," the pretty blonde said.

"I've half a mind to ship your entire establishment to Connecticut," Janet said.

"Oh, dear. That would never do. How would I ever keep Syd busy?" Scott chuckled. "She would get into trouble. I'm sure of it."

"I'll take Sydney as well."

Scott laughed as he made his way to his chair and dropped into it heavily. "In that case, we may be able to come to terms."

The two women started to talk. Syd pulled her chair up close to Scott. "I need to clear my head. You mind if I take a ride?"

Concern colored his face. "Something bothering you?"

"You could say something's bothering me. Your friend from the other day came in. I guess he's feeling better."

"The gentleman who had the heart attack?"

"You guessed it in one."

"What did he want?"

"What do you think he wanted?"

"To thank you for saving his life? Maybe show his appreciation in the form of a gift. Something in a small box from Tiffany's perhaps."

"Yeah, like that was likely." She leaned closer to whisper into his ear. "He wanted *that fucking book!*" She stood up and brightened her tone of voice. "So I'm taking Phoenix out for a ride to blow the stink off me."

"That's fine. I'll take care of these delightful women all by myself."

"Do you want me to bring you some dinner back?"

"No, I prefer my sustenance without windburn."

"Suit yourself. I'll be back in an hour or so."

She withdrew her leather jacket and a helmet painted to resemble a fierce bird out from behind the counter then sprang for the door. Minutes later, she broke free of the city traffic and rode Phoenix down a little-used two-lane road. The bike howled between her legs as she unwound the speedometer.

Wind rushed by, and her thoughts turned to *that fucking book*. It hadn't interested the gay woman, a serious collector. She'd walked past it dozens of times, never sparing it a glance. The soon-to-be-married Gopher, on the other hand, probably hadn't read anything other than menus in years. Nevertheless, it had spoken to him. Then there was the heart attack victim. One near-death experience, and he was back for more.

Sydney didn't believe in the supernatural, but she didn't have an explanation either. *I've got to chase this shit out of my head.* She had spent more than a few nights drinking coffee while researching the origins of that unusual volume. There were innumerable legends about books with magical powers—grimoires, bibles, pagan religious texts, and occultism. Some warned of dire consequences if opened with the wrong intentions. Others could not be opened at all unless specific conditions were met. Others were bound with human skin and said to contain the secret of immortality. Not one was said to be blank, whimsically revealing itself only to chosen individuals.

Halfway through a tight turn, she spotted a layer of sand that had blown across the road. Her muscles bunched. She backed off the accelerator and straightened the bike. The tires slewed to the side, and Syd fought for balance. It was all up to Phoenix. Syd gave her the lead. Overcontrolling the skid would spell disaster.

Phoenix crossed the centerline, and Syd prepared to lay her down. The soft shoulder approached as the sand tapered away. Changing her plan, Syd leaned hard to her right, downshifted, and rolled the accelerator. Phoenix responded with a guttural roar. They could still make the turn.

The long blast from an air horn shattered her focus. The chrome grill of a Peterbilt bore down on her, and she had to choose—death or desert. She changed the direction of the bike again, passing the right front fender of the truck close enough to kiss. The hot rush of air from the passing truck nudged her off the blacktop. Phoenix shot into the desert, and her front tire sank into the soft sand. Syd flew over the handlebars and braced for the inevitable rush of pain.

Sudden silence struck her when she stopped bouncing. Sitting up with care, she glanced at a particularly nasty cactus on her left. "Could've been worse."

Slowly, she stood, taking inventory. "Two legs, check. Two arms, check. Pulling my head out of my ass, check, check. The gang's all here. Nice of the truck driver to hang around. What a dick."

Gingerly, she walked back to Phoenix and surveyed the damage. It was mostly cosmetic. If all that was needed was a little touch-up, she would log this one in the win column. They'd both risen from the ashes of real wrecks in the past, which she had documented in ink on her skin. She would be adding a small one to commemorate this little brush with the reaper. Maybe she would sketch a stylized grill of the Peterbilt. A couple bruises and some paint wouldn't require much of a tattoo.

When Syd finally got Phoenix back on the road, the bike roared to life. Saguaros cast long shadows, and the sun angled toward the horizon. Scott would be worrying. She hated the thought of making him worry. While she wasn't looking, he had carved out a room in her heart. She realized she loved the incorrigible old reprobate, and it pained her to think that she had given him cause for concern. Hot air dried her sweat-drenched body as she leaned into the last of the turns. Soon, she would be negotiating the city traffic.

Her stomach growled, and a horn made her jump. Unaware she'd been sitting through a green light, she squealed the tire, pulling out onto Scottsdale Road. One block later, she turned into the parking lot of Alcuin Books. She tucked Phoenix in beside Scott's old Subaru, shut her down, and listened to the engine cool. After pulling her helmet off, she swiped at a tear forming in her eye. Understanding flooded through her. She would not be leaving this town because she was home at last. A real home. Her home. *Besides, who would take care of the hopeless old scoundrel if I left?*

"Are you going to sit out there all night?" Scott asked from the doorway.

"Don't get your panties in a bunch. I'm coming." She cleared emotion from her voice then threw her aching leg over the bike.

"Didn't you say you'd only be gone one hour? You better get a watch, woman." He smiled and stepped aside to let her pass then locked the door behind her. "Aside from the missing paint on poor Phoenix, you don't look any worse for wear."

"Just a zigging problem." Syd waited for him to get back to his chair.

He wheezed as he took his seat. "I can only presume you were zagging at the time."

"Yeah, that's the gist of it."

"It's a good thing you didn't have your cell phone with

you." He lifted it off his desk. "It might have been damaged."

"Yeah, they're just a distraction when the shit is hitting the fan." She held her hand out.

Scott placed it back on his desk. "Did you eat?"

"Not since lunch with Johnny Walker."

"That's fine. Good nutrition in alcohol." He picked up the phone and dialed.

Syd stowed her helmet. "So how—"

Scott held up a finger. "Yes, good evening, Tony. Can you send over a Sydney for me? Thank you."

"I'm perfectly capable of ordering my own dinner, you know."

"Why do you bristle when I do something thoughtful for you?"

She shrugged. The too-close call had flattened her defenses. "I still have a hard time accepting that people will do anything without an ulterior motive."

"It will please you, no doubt, to know I too have covert reasons for being nice to you. Our coffers are running over, thanks to Janet, who gushed over how wonderful you were."

"That's the job, not that it pays much." She smiled. He compensated her well, but she had an obligation to bitch about her pay. It was the universal responsibility of employees everywhere.

Scott steepled his fingers. "The current trend is to reduce wages and benefits. Would you like to open a formal negotiation?"

"Nah, it's late. Maybe tomorrow." She grabbed a bottle of water from the mini fridge and a couple of Advil from Scott's desk.

He gestured to the seat across from him. "I thought we might talk about something we can disagree on."

She laughed. "You want to narrow that down a little?"

"Specifically, the existence of agencies not easily explained away."

Her empty stomach did a flip. "Not *that fucking book*?" A knock at the door stopped her.

"That will be Tony with your dinner."

When she returned with her sandwich, she noticed that a somber demeanor had settled over Scott.

"You eat whilst I pontificate. You will agree that knowledge is power."

She nodded with a mouthful of sausage and peppers then wiped at a string of cheese dangling from her chin.

"Responsibility must accompany knowledge." Scott opened a file drawer. "With great knowledge comes—"

"Great responsibility. Get on with it." Syd took another bite.

Scott laid a thick file on his desk. "This comprises everything I know about the volume in question. It also contains many things I suspect but can't prove. I have more than one working theory regarding the mysteries surrounding *The Harbinger*."

"Why do you call it that?"

"It's not ladylike to talk with your mouth full."

She swallowed. "You'll be relieved to know I'm no lady. Continue."

He patted the file. "What isn't in here is my deference to the power *The Harbinger* wields nor the trepidation I have over the abuses it could be put to. In short, I fear it may fall into the wrong hands. I have become the unfortunate guardian of this vile artifact."

"First of all, I can't begin to believe—"

"I'm not asking you to believe in anything right now. I'm asking you to keep an open mind as you read my notes." He handed the file over. "At the risk of sounding dramatic, this is for your eyes only."

She hefted it to her lap and opened it. The table of contents didn't surprise her. She knew too well Scott's penchant for organization. "I don't know quite what to say. Should I be pissed because you've kept this from me for two years or honored you trust me with it?"

"Neither. If you understood what you're getting yourself into, you'd hop on Phoenix and never look back."

"Can I ask a stupid question?"

"I doubt I could stop you if I tried."

"If it's so dangerous, why don't you lock it up somewhere safe?"

"That's a very good question. It seems that the entity—that is, *The Harbinger*—needs to be viewed. Over the years, men who have used the book and attempted to lock it away to keep it for themselves have suffered great tragedy. For that reason, I keep it in a place where it can be seen. If it remains contented and in the hands of a benign guardian —and this is supposition on my part—it remains mostly harmless." The effort he exerted to stand came out in the form of a groan. "Try not to stay up all night reading. I'll see you in the morning."

She followed him to the door. "You be careful driving home."

"It's two blocks. I'll manage." He ruffled her hair. "I know how much you dislike that, but humor an old man."

She locked up after him, turned off the lights, and took the file to the back room. She read while preparing the coffee maker. She cleared her desk, and she read. Fragrant coffee blossomed into the air, and she read. On a legal pad, she scribbled notes she wanted to fact-check, and she read.

According to Scott's notes, the earliest account of

anything resembling The *Harbinger* occurred in the form of a scroll in the hands of Julius Caesar.

"(Impossible to confirm) Writings from antiquity report that Julius Caesar had a blank scroll that advised him to (among other things) refuse the crown of Emperor until the commoners of Rome insisted he accept."

What followed were a list of references to mysterious documents capable of prophesizing the future and influencing historical figures, including Herod Antipas, King of Judea; Macbeth, King of Scots; and Osman Ghazi, the first Ottoman Sultan. All were legend in nature with no hard evidence to support Scott's suspicions. What really piqued her interest were the entries that described the book she knew all too well in detail down to the blank pages.

In 1434, Gutenberg had such a book with diagrams for movable type, which led to his inventing the printing press. There was an anecdote that he was so tormented by the blank pages, he spilled ink on them.

Scott had noted, *"The Harbinger isn't always a bad influence. Gutenberg's invention led to an information explosion and increased literacy. Which led to the Age of Enlightenment and the Reformation."*

The next reference pertained to John Locke's *Leviathan.* The implication was that his treatise on liberty, progress, tolerance, fraternity, constitutional government, and separation of church and state were influenced by *The Harbinger,* which in turn influenced rebellions against monarchies across the continent, including the Russian, American, and French Revolutions.

"And all of those events led to a great deal of bloodshed and suffering as well as two democracies and the great socialist experiment. The knowledge in this book always wields a double-edged sword."

Adolf Hitler had possessed a similar tome that disappeared in Berlin. It was rumored to have been in the possession of Thomas Edison, who had the book until it disappeared when Henry Ford left the Edison Illumination Company to start the Ford Motor Company.

Syd woke with a stiff neck. Drool stained the corner of Scott's file. The clutter in residence on her desk stood witness to her night's endeavors. "Coffee. Must have strong coffee."

It was six a.m., and the ridiculously cheerful baristas at Starbucks would be unlocking the doors. She was stiff and sore and still wearing the clothes she'd had on yesterday. *I need to stretch my legs, and some fresh air wouldn't hurt either.*

The cool early-morning air felt good as she walked the one block to Starbucks. She thought of the book as *The Harbinger* now, and for good reason. Scott believed if *The Harbinger* spoke to someone, his or her life was about to change, whether for good or bad. It seemed to be up to the receiver of the message and how they utilized what they read. Scott had recorded events that had gone both ways. *Christ, but that's frightening, and I'm only halfway through.* The documentation improved as the timeline moved forward. She had a lot of research to do.

"Hey, Syd." Karen greeted her from behind the espresso machine. "The usual?"

"Make it two, Karen."

"Two venti five-shot Americanos, Charlie." Karen rang up the order. "Rough night?"

"Nah, just reading." Syd ran a hand through her hair. "Requirement of the job. You know, bookstore and all."

"Anytime you want to switch, let me know."

"Not in this lifetime." Syd rehashed the events she'd recently witnessed while the espresso machine hissed and gurgled. The soon-to-be-married Gopher had received wedding vows. *How could that go bad?* She shuddered when she thought of the men in her mother's life. Then there was the heart attack guy. *What did the book say to him?*

Karen slid the carrier over. "See you later?"

"Yeah, later." Syd hurried back. She fumbled with the key, opened the door, then locked herself in. Standing at the pedestal, she stared at *The Harbinger*. If half of what she'd read last night were true, this book should be feared.

She flipped it open to a random page. The carrier dropped from her hand, and two Americanos exploded upon impact.

I, Scott Hendrickson, being of sound mind and body, do bequeath all my worldly possessions to Sydney Steinert...

Wolves Of Karma

S pencer Quinn paced his opulent penthouse office, pausing to look onto Fifth Avenue and steeling himself for a video conference call with Japan that could turn into a lucrative deal. Dealing with the Japanese was a big pain in the ass. This preliminary call wouldn't accomplish much, if anything at all. He anticipated a lot of posturing. A little groveling was the price of doing business in Japan. It stuck in Spencer's craw and did nothing to improve his usual bad temper.

Down on the street, a man in a denim jacket and long hair held a sign, *The Wolves of Karma are coming for you.* He wore a quality wolf mask, and Spencer couldn't take his eyes off him. The sign was poised above his head and angled directly at Quinn's office.

From the phone, his personal assistant interrupted his thoughts. "Mr. Quinn?"

"What is it, Doris?"

"Mr. Grant would like a couple minutes of your time, sir."

"Is he smiling?"

"Like the Cheshire Cat, sir."

"Send him in."

"Just a reminder, your conference call with Japan starts in six minutes."

"I'm aware. Send him in." Quinn continued staring out the window. *This had better be good news.*

Joey Grant closed the door and cleared his throat nervously. "Mr. Quinn, thanks for taking the time, sir."

"You have something for me, Grant?" Quinn asked without turning around.

"I just heard from my contact at the city. The property in Queens, the Madison Hotel, has defaulted on their taxes. Harry Brewer over at First City Bank confirmed the insurance policy lapsed, and the bank has already started processing the paper to foreclose. It should be on auction by the end of the month."

"What an idiot."

"Sir?"

"Not you, Grant. Look at this guy." He motioned Grant to the window.

Grant walked over and peered down onto Fifth Avenue. "Who am I looking at, sir?"

"The guy on the corner, wearing the mask."

"The one holding the sign?"

"Do you see another guy in a mask?" Quinn turned away from the window to look at Grant.

"I don't see anyone in a mask, Mr. Quinn."

"He's holding that sign over his head and pointing it up." Quinn turned back. The sign blocked the man's face. "Yes. The one with the sign. Who the fuck is going to see that besides me?"

Grant scoffed. "Not the best marketing stratagem."

"You think? Is there some crackpot off-Broadway show about werewolves?"

"Not that I know of." Grant moved closer to the window. "'The Wolves of Karma are coming for you.'"

"I can read." Quinn huffed. "But who are they coming for?"

Grant backed away from the window. "Must be a show, like you said."

"If a show needs a gimmick, it's already doomed to close." Quinn turned and pinned Grant with a look. "You were saying something about the property in Queens."

"Yes. My guy at the bank said it should be up for auction by the end of the month."

"Call him back. I'm not bidding against a bunch of obstructionists. Those fucking liberal do-gooders would have the city decay around them rather than allow me to develop the area into something useful. Tell your banker I'll buy the note out and clear up the back taxes if he's willing to forego the auction. Can you make that happen, Grant?"

"I think Harry would be willing to cut through some red tape for us. It may cost us a Caribbean vacation, sir. There's nothing like a New York City February to entice someone into bending the rules."

"Do it. And Grant?" He waited until Grant turned. "That makes you the first to reach double digits this year."

Grant's grin broadened until it resembled that of a great white shark. "Keeping the streak alive."

Quinn walked to his wet bar. "What streak is that?"

"Second year in a row I closed out ten properties first."

"I'm not sure two constitutes a streak." Quinn turned from the bar to face Grant. "Maybe you're just lucky. I'm sure the boiler explosion and fire had something to do with your recent good fortune."

"I'm sure you're right, sir." Grant held his hands out,

palms up, and shrugged. "Sometimes it's better to be lucky than good."

"Go, call your guy. Get me that property today, and you can join your banker in the Caribbean."

Grant practically skipped out of Quinn's office.

Quinn poured bourbon from a crystal decanter. Swirling the liquor, he turned back to the window. If he didn't know that no one could see into his window, he would swear the guy in the mask was looking right at him.

Ignoring a frisson of unease, he turned away and perched one ass cheek on the front of the desk while composing his I-don't-give-a-fuck face for the videoconference about to begin. The large video screen on the opposite wall flickered to life early, drawing his ire. He hadn't switched it on yet. The tumbler of bourbon slipped from his fingers as he gaped at the screen.

A wolf stared from the monitor. Eyes of liquid amber gave the fierce expression of hunger. "The Wolves of Karma are coming for *you*, Quinn," it snarled. Then the screen went blank.

"What the fuck?" Quinn burst from his office. "Doris, move my call to the conference room. No video. Then get IT up here, stat. Tell them to check everything. Someone fucking hacked our system. Get maintenance to clean the carpet in my office and tell Lester to meet me in the conference room. *Now*."

Quinn was down the hall before she could respond. A patina of sweat covered his face, and his heart pounded in his chest. When he reached the conference room, Lester was waiting for him.

The man rose from his chair when Quinn barged into the room. "Hey, boss, are you all right? Doris said something about being hacked."

Lester followed Quinn as he moved to the window.

Quinn struggled to control his breathing and keep his voice level. The sign blocked his face again. "You see the guy on the corner, holding up the sign?"

"I got him in my crosshairs." Lester's slow Midwestern drawl could be infuriating at times. And this was one of those times. "What about him?"

"Put somebody on him. I want to know everything, from his mother's maiden name to the color of his last shit. You got it?"

"No problemo, Boss. Does this have something to do with the hack?"

"No. I decided to harass some jerk-off on the corner for no apparent reason. Just get it done."

Cell phone in hand, Lester turned away without another word.

The phone in the conference room beeped softly. Quinn hit the hands-free button. "Yes."

"Your conference call with Tokyo is waiting on line two, Mr. Quinn."

He took several deep breaths to compose his anger and hit the blinking button, but he kept his gaze on the figure standing on the corner below. "Quinn here."

Two men in expensive suits approached the guy holding the sign. What appeared to be a civil conversation ensued until a white, unmarked utility van pulled to the curb. Two men emerged from the van and joined the first two. Four of them threw Sign Man into the van and jumped in behind him. The door closed, and the van pulled into traffic. The sign lay on the sidewalk, angled so Quinn could still read it.

Quinn sucked in a breath. *Christ, Lester, that seems a little severe.* He turned his attention back to the conference call. These tedious preliminary meetings bored him to distraction. *The way the Japs talk, you'd think that fucking island was covered in gold instead of nuclear waste and rice paddies. Too bad that tsunami didn't wash the rock completely clean.*

With this round of "We'll look into that" and "We're considering other offers" in the books, he hung up and made his way back to his office. A dozen men were crawling around with a fortune in testing equipment strewn about.

The head of IT spotted him and came over. "Mr. Quinn, can you tell me why you think we've been hacked? I'm seeing nothing to indicate we've had a breach."

"Well, look harder. The video screen came on by itself. Some guy in wolf makeup spoke, and then it went off again. I never touched it."

"What did this guy say?"

"You tell me, and you'll still have a job next week." He turned to Doris. "Have my car brought around. I'll be working from home until we get this sorted out."

"Should I cancel your schedule?" Doris asked.

"What do you think?" Quinn prowled to his personal elevator. His hand shook as he pressed the button for the garage. When the floor dropped from under him, he braced himself in the corner, pressing his hands against perpendicular walls. It was the fastest elevator in the world. He was accustomed to the speed, but today it startled him. When his stomach returned to its rightful position, the doors opened. When Quinn saw Ted, his driver, waiting for him, he relaxed and blew out a breath.

With Ted's tan face, blond buzz cut, and brick-shit-house stature, he looked as if he'd stepped right off the cover of *Soldier of Fortune* magazine. Quinn walked to the open door of the limo.

"Where to, Mr. Quinn?"

"Home, Ted. I need a workout." He slid into the luxurious back seat. Ted closed the door and drove smoothly into midtown traffic. He poured himself a bourbon to replace the one currently soaking into the carpet in his office. His phone vibrated. "Yes, Doris?"

"Mr. Grant is here. He would like another word."

"Tell him to stop wasting your time and send an email. No more calls, Doris. No exceptions." He terminated the call and settled into the leather seat. The hand raising the glass to his lips shook with a mild tremor. When his eyes closed, he could still see the wolf face as clear as if the wolf were sitting across from him. The creepy yellow eyes, the hunger, and the gravel-coated voice filled his head. "Wolves of Karma? Let's see what kind of karma you're experiencing in Lester's interrogation room."

Quinn hit the intercom button to speak to Ted. "Change in plans. Head over to Kent Avenue."

"Brooklyn, sir?"

"Yes, under the Williamsburg Bridge."

"I know the location."

"ETA?"

"Forty minutes, sir."

Quinn sent an email to his own hacker, a first-rate ball buster but excellent at what he did. "*Be at the bridge in forty minutes.*" Paranoid didn't come close to describing the man he knew only as Kraken. All conversation had to be in person. Kraken would only accept payment in cash and nothing larger than well-circulated twenty-dollar bills.

The response was almost immediate. "*Make it fifty or wait.*"

"*See you in fifty,*" he emailed back.

The lighter-than-usual traffic put Quinn in Brooklyn early. "Go around the block, Ted. We're ten minutes early." From the comfort of his limo, he observed the gentrification that had slowly spread through Brooklyn like a creeping vine. Small businesses were renovating once-abandoned buildings. Health food stores and boutiques had moved in. Former hippies who'd made the transition to respectable business owners sat around in coffee shops, sipping lattes.

Ted finally pulled over at a bus stop under the Williamsburg Bridge and slipped out of the car. The yuppies and their urban redevelopment hadn't reached the old whore stroll under the bridge yet. Later that night, it would be replete with junkies and prostitutes. Ted unbuttoned his suit coat and stood like a sentinel next to the limo. Quinn watched him scan the activity on the street, vigilant for any sign of trouble.

A young man with long, greasy hair, wearing a dirty Yankees hoody, approached the car. "Hey, Teddy, how ya doin'?"

Ted nodded and opened the limo door.

Kraken slid into the rear-facing seat of Quinn's limo. "Big D, how many people have you crushed today?"

Quinn flinched at the moniker. He disliked the nickname and Kraken's familiarity. "I've done all right. How many lives have you ruined today?"

"From the look on your face, I'm at least one short." Kraken's smile revealed yellowing teeth. "What can I do for the all-powerful Daddy Warbucks machine today?"

"I was threatened. They hacked into the building communications with a video feed to my office."

"Whoa, that's magical hacking right there. I ought to know since I designed your firewalls." Kraken scratched his three-day-old beard. "Before I set the electronic wilderness ablaze, you got any clues for me?"

"A guy in werewolf makeup said, 'The Wolves of Karma are coming for you, Quinn.'"

"Wolves of Karma? That's catchy. I'll handle it."

Quinn opened a console in the door. "The usual arrangement?"

Kraken held up his hand. "Save it. The first twenty-four hours are on the house."

Quinn looked up with an envelope in his hand. "Seriously?"

"I'll find these wolves for free because they had the effrontery to piss on my turf. There's a price for going where no man has gone before. Ask Captain Kirk about that. When I know who they are, the usual rates will apply. But believe me when I say they will be bleeding from every orifice before we're done with them."

Quinn smiled, opened the envelope, and took two banded stacks of twenties out. He fanned them for Kraken to prove the bills had been well-circulated. "Take this anyway, call it a show of good faith."

Kraken shrugged and accepted the bills. He fanned them again then reached into his back pocket and pulled out an old flip phone. "I like how you roll, D. Take this. It's a burner. I'll be in touch."

"You have a charger for this relic?" Quinn asked.

That elicited a hearty laugh from Kraken that propelled his bad breath across the car. "This whole thing will be a distant memory before you need a charge." He stuffed the bills inside his shirt and reached for the door. "In the meantime, keep your head down."

Quinn watched as Kraken got out and disappeared around a corner. Ted slipped behind the wheel and drove to Quinn's mansion on the Upper East Side.

"Welcome home, Mr. Quinn. You're early." Victor took

Quinn's overcoat with a manicured hand. "Can I prepare a refreshment for you?"

"No. You can get a hold of the worthless piece of shit living in my guesthouse and tell him to meet me in the gym."

"I hope you don't mind me asking, but since everyone seems to agree that Tony is, as you say, a worthless piece of shit, why is he still here?"

Quinn grinned. "Because I get a certain amount of satisfaction from kicking the shit out of him."

Tony was his ex-wife's son from a previous marriage, and his stay was supposed to have been temporary. It had started as a simple favor for his ex, but Tony had over-stayed his welcome. Quinn did enjoy sparring with the kid. When he smacked Camille's precious Tony around, the alimony hurt a little less. Before Tony moved in, Quinn had sparred with Victor. During their sessions together, Victor had barely broken a sweat. And although Quinn was sure Victor had pulled his punches, Quinn would come away bruised and battered.

"Very well. I'll see to it."

"And Victor, no calls tonight unless *you* deem them important."

Victor turned sharply on his heel and left the spacious foyer for parts unknown. Quinn figured everyone from Victor down to the housekeeper would like a piece of Tony. He had no doubt that Mrs. Weaver would kick Tony's ass. She was a tough old broad who probably resented the job of cleaning up after the kid in the guesthouse.

Tony, a former UFC wannabe, gave Quinn the oppor-tunity to put the day behind him as they exchanged blows. There was no room for daydreaming in the octagon. After sparring with Tony, Quinn hit the sauna and took a cold shower.

Finally, Quinn made his way to the library.

Victor arrived right behind him with a crystal tumbler of bourbon. "Dinner?"

"I'll take it in here." Quinn sank into a chair and clicked on his news feeds. A wall slid apart, revealing eight large flat screens, each tuned to a different news source. He sipped his drink and scanned the stock exchange until the local station caught his attention. They were showing an aerial view of a white van. He clicked off the mute.

"That's right, Charles, the police have cordoned off four blocks of Manhattan at rush hour to investigate this particularly brutal crime scene."

"We have a shot of the van up right now, Percy. Can you tell us what we're seeing?"

"It's hard to make out from your vantage point, Charles, but the van looks like a slaughterhouse. Blood and body parts are strewn everywhere. The NYPD believes there to be as many as four victims, who were quite literally torn to shreds inside the van. Seasoned homicide detectives have turned away from the scene, shaken and looking a little green around the gills. The working theory is that these three or four individuals were illegally transporting some wild animal that got away from them. Residents are being advised to stay inside until the authorities can track and contain whatever it was that tore these men to unidentifiable pieces."

"What steps are the authorities taking to safeguard the citizens of New York, Percy?"

"They've advised everyone to get indoors and stay there. All available helicopters are lighting up the immediate area. The authorities have animal control as well as experts from the zoo standing by.

Forensic teams are poring over the scene in an attempt to identify exactly what they're looking for."

The shot changed to the studio. "That was Percy Martinez reporting from the scene for Spectrum News, NY1, keeping you up to date on…"

Quinn muted the television and dialed Lester's cell.

"I'm a little busy just now, boss." Lester's normally soft-spoken, easygoing Midwestern drawl was gone, a taut, strained voice in its place.

"They were your men? The ones I'm seeing on the news?"

"Yes, and they were good men, boss. Some of the best I've ever worked with."

"Let me know when you have anything at all."

"You betcha." Lester disconnected.

Victor came in with a tray of food that filled the spacious library with mouthwatering aromas.

"If Lester calls, put him through, no matter what hour." Quinn drank the rest of his bourbon. "You might as well enjoy that, Victor." He motioned to his dinner. "I won't be eating tonight."

"You look awfully pale. Should I put a call in to your doctor?"

"I'm fine." Quinn ran a hand through his hair. "There're problems at the office." He held up his empty glass. "Bring the decanter."

Victor set down the tray of food, retrieved the bourbon, and poured for Quinn. "Do you want some company while you wait for Lester to call back?"

"That would be fine, but get this out of here first." He pushed the tray of food away. "And bring yourself a glass."

Victor nodded and retreated, taking the tray of food with him.

All eight monitors momentarily switched to a blue

screen. Then one at a time, they came back to life, filled with the profile of a wolf's head. Quinn stood as eight images of the wolf turned to look at him. The liquid amber eyes bored straight into Quinn's soul. The snout was coated in gore. Blood dripped from its mouth as it spoke. "Quinn, the Wolves of Karma are coming for *you*." The tongue flicked out and licked along its snout.

"Fuck you!" Quinn threw his tumbler at one of the screens. The image fractured, and the glass stuck there, mocking him.

Victor ran into the library with a handgun held stiffly at his side. "Mr. Quinn!" He scanned the room for intruders. "What is it?"

Quinn pointed at Victor's weapon. "I'm expecting company. Keep that handy."

"Of course." Victor glanced at his Beretta. "Who are we expecting?"

"Sit down. Pour yourself a drink." Quinn reached into one of his desk drawers and pulled out a beautifully crafted wooden box. He opened it to reveal a pistol with a flat black finish highlighted by a touch of brass on the handle. From the box, it screamed unparalleled workmanship. Quinn knew the pistol's appearance was second only to the way it performed in his grip. The 1911 .45 from Jesse James Firearms in Texas was perfectly balanced and customized for him. An expression flickered across Victor's face. Quinn wasn't sure if it was admiration or surprise. He inspected the weapon, loaded the clip, then slapped it in place. Finally, he racked a shell into the chamber.

"Mr. Quinn, do you mind telling me who we're waiting for?"

"The Wolves of Karma."

Victor winced. "Are you sure you're feeling all right?"

Quinn reiterated the pertinent details of his day for

Victor, ending with the old-fashioned crystal glass lodged in the video screen. "I would have expected Lester to have filled you in."

"Sounds like Lester's been busy." Victor slipped his cell phone from his jacket pocket. "There's been a threat. Lock down the property. No one comes in without my say-so. Call in additional staff. Take whatever measures you deem necessary." After a pause, he responded, "Would I be calling you if this weren't serious? Extreme measures. You understand?" He terminated the call.

Quinn always knew Victor to be a serious man. It was the reason he'd hired him in the first place. Over the ensuing years, Victor had taken on the role of managing Quinn's home as well as his security. For the first time since Joey Grant had come into his office that morning, Quinn grinned. "I couldn't help but notice you forgot to tell him what the threat was."

"I want them on their toes. If I told them to be on the lookout for a wolf, they'd think I'd lost it."

"Thank you, Victor."

Victor nodded and pushed another button on his phone. "Ted, join Mr. Quinn and me in the library, please. Bring some of your toys to the party." He splashed a little bourbon into a glass. "As many as you want."

Quinn looked on as control of his life slipped through his fingers.

Victor held up his phone. "Shall I bring Lester up to speed?"

"Go ahead. I'll clear out some e-mails."

Victor moved around the room. He looked out each window, checking the perimeter, while he talked softly to Lester.

Quinn fired up his computer and logged into his secure e-mail account. Immediately, his eyes were drawn to the extraordinary number of unread e-mails, the majority of which had come from Joey Grant. The subject lines read, "*Wolves of Karma.*"

He clicked on the most recent.

"*Where the fuck are you, Quinn? These fuckers mean to kill me.*"

He scrolled back to the earliest e-mail from Grant.

"*Hey, that wolf thing just hit my terminal. I called IT, but I thought you'd want to know.*"

From there, Grant's panic could be tracked as it mounted exponentially with each message.

Quinn clicked reply. "*Grant, Sorry, I've been busy. Where are you now? Are you safe?*"

He turned his attention back to the local news and waited for Grant's reply. Spectrum News had a crackerjack team for a local station. They already had a graphic for "The Wild Animal Attacks."

"More than one?" Quinn muttered and clicked off the mute.

"*Stay inside and lock your doors. NYPD is now reporting two additional attacks in the Borough of Manhattan. One moment.*" The anchor put a hand to his ear and tilted his head like a dog catching some unusual sound. "*I've been informed we have identified one of the victims.*" A driver's license photo of Joey Grant filled half the screen. "*One Joseph Sherman Grant of…*"

Quinn muted the audio again. "Victor!" His trembling hand pointed at the screen. "Ask Lester what he knows about this." He retrieved another tumbler from the armoire and poured a generous drink.

Victor stared at the screen, which was dominated by the image of Joseph Sherman Grant. Color drained from his face. Quinn walked over to Victor and put a hand on his shoulder. "Ask him if his contacts know who the other victim is."

Victor relayed the question. "The second was Harold Brewer, a VP at First City Bank."

"Jesus!" Quinn rocked on his feet. "That's Grant's contact."

Victor held his phone out to Quinn. "He wants to talk to you."

"Yes, Lester?"

"How does Grant figure into this?"

"Joey was working on a project for me."

"What project?"

"We're buying up a city block in Queens. A residential hotel was the last holdout. Joey's guy at First City Bank was expediting the deal."

Lester's voice tightened. "The name of the hotel?"

"The Madison. It's a fleabag full of drunks and drug addicts."

"Many of them were also Vietnam vets who never transitioned back into the world."

Quinn's mouth went dry. He walked to his desk and lifted his glass. "Lester?"

There was a noticeable pause before Lester spoke. "The fire. How many died in that blaze, Quinn?"

Quinn heard the implication loud and clear. "I don't know! There was a boiler explosion. I had nothing to do with it!" He hated the defensive tone in his voice. He would never admit it, but he was sure Joey Grant had everything to do with that boiler explosion that had resulted in a tragic fire. He didn't know how many had died, nor had he cared until this moment. Victor's green eyes watched him closely.

Another pause, this one longer, stretched out before Lester spoke again. "Put Victor back on."

Quinn handed Victor's cell back just as Ted strolled into the library, carrying a black nylon duffle. He looked even more intimidating out of the suit he wore when driving Quinn's car. The snug black T-shirt, cargo pants, and running shoes accented his no-nonsense demeanor. Victor pointed him to a table under a window as he listened to Lester.

Ted removed a soft cloth from the bag and spread it out over the table. He hummed as he removed one weapon at a time. Carefully, he inspected each piece before loading it and arranging it on the table. When Victor joined him, they talked softly.

Quinn cleared his throat. "I'd like to be included in any discussion regarding my life, if you don't mind."

Victor turned sharply. "We're discussing who else might be in harm's way if, as you indicated, it's connected with the Madison Hotel fire." Victor walked over to Quinn. "Have a seat, sir. Let us handle this. Ted mentioned you met with that whacko in Brooklyn today. Can you reach him? Maybe he knows something."

"He gave me a burner." Quinn pulled the flip phone from his inside jacket pocket and placed it on his desk.

"Shall we see what he knows?"

Quinn bit back his rising anger at Victor's tone. First Lester, and now Victor. Some changes would be made around here when this blew over. He emailed Kraken. "*Call me.*" Then he waited.

Victor pointed at the phone against his ear. "Tony's not picking up, so Ted's going out to the casita. He's going to tell Tony to clear out for a few days." Again, this was a statement, not a question. Victor waved Ted off.

Ted shouldered an assault rifle in addition to his sidearm for the twenty-yard walk to the casita.

When they were alone, Victor sat in a chair facing Quinn's desk and slid Quinn's fancy pistol out of reach.

"How about we leave the shooting to the professionals tonight."

Quinn waved a hand at the table loaded with Ted's toys. "That's an awful lot of hardware."

"It's better to have and not need than to need and not have."

Quinn leaned his head back and closed his eyes. The adrenaline rush from earlier was wearing off, and exhaustion settled like a great weight. "I'm placing myself in your most competent hands, Victor. Is Lester joining us?"

"Not right away. He's doing some reconnaissance. Lester has his own agenda right now. We've beefed up the exterior crew. They should be able to handle anything that comes their way. On the off chance someone gets past them"—Victor nodded toward the arsenal on the table —"Ted and I will be here."

When the flip phone chirped on his desk, Quinn snatched it up and switched to the speaker. "Thank God you're still alive. Have you seen the news? Do you have anything yet? It's getting tense around here." Quinn heard harsh breathing. "Are you there?"

"Yes, Quinn. We are here." That familiar rusty voice bored into his head. "The Wolves of Karma have been busy tonight. But we haven't forgotten about you. We are coming."

Quinn dropped the phone to the desktop.

Victor snatched it up with lightning reflexes. "Who's calling, please?" He paused. "Answer me!"

"Quinn knows who's calling. My advice, don't be there when we arrive." The call terminated.

Victor looked at the phone. "Was that your hacker buddy?"

"Of course not." Quinn's voice shook as he spoke. "He's probably dead."

"You don't know that."

Quinn mopped sweat from his brow.

"Mr. Quinn, look at me." Victor waited a beat. "Spencer!"

Quinn looked into Victor's penetrating green eyes at the sound of his given name. "What is it?"

"Don't jump to conclusions. Stay with me on this. This whole thing could have been orchestrated by... what's his name, the hacker?"

"Kraken. That's his handle, or whatever they call it."

"Fucking Kraken. Have you considered this might be him? He certainly has the skills to get into your secure communications. And interrupting the signal here would be child's play for him." Victor went to the window, scratching his head. "I never liked you doing business with that guy in the first place."

"Sure, he could do the tech stuff, but the violence, that's not his style. Emptying my bank accounts electronically? Yes. But not this."

"How can you be so sure?"

"I've been appraising people and property for twenty-five years. I know. He's not a get-your-hands-dirty kind of guy."

"Maybe he picked up a partner recently." Even Victor's usual polish seemed to be tarnishing a little. "Someone willing to do the wet work."

"I don't think anyone gets past the handle. He's strictly a solo act. He's too fucking paranoid to trust anyone."

"That's Ted's read on him too." Victor held up his hand and slid his phone from his jacket pocket. "Go, Ted." Victor mouthed the words "no Tony" to Quinn. "Where is he? All right, don't worry about it. Yes. Just get back here."

"What's going on with Tony?" Quinn asked.

"The worthless piece of shit evidently packed a bag in

a hurry and left. I don't guess he mentioned anything to you during your workout?"

"No, he didn't. It's not like him to go anywhere without asking for a handout. Now there's a guy I don't trust. That's why he's in the guesthouse. He might try something like this."

Victor nodded and raised his phone again. "I want a workup on Anthony Watson, all known associates as well as his current location. Anytime in the last ten minutes will do."

Quinn looked at the man whose hands he had placed his life into. "Who was that?"

"A friend of mine at Homeland. If Tony's working with someone, we'll know soon."

Ted walked in and handed a piece of paper to Victor. "What do you make of that?"

Victor passed it to Quinn. A hastily written message was scrawled across the page. *"I don't know whose bed you shit in this time, but good luck. Tony"*

Quinn balled it up and threw it. "Typical."

Ted ran a hand over his blond buzz cut. "You think someone got to him, Captain?"

"Hard to say. I've got Suresh working him up already."

"I saw Chef in the kitchen. Told him to go home."

Victor looked stricken. "Christ, I forgot he was still here. I could have used some coffee."

Ted smiled. "Got you covered, Captain."

As if it were choreographed on Broadway, Chef trundled in, pushing a cart full of goodies that was dominated by a large silver urn. He nodded to Mr. Quinn, and his almond-shaped eyes grew too large for his face when he noticed the array of weapons. "Anything else, Mr. Victor?"

Victor stood and walked over to the cart. "Thank you, Giang. We're dealing with a situation. Take tomorrow off."

He nodded. "Yes, sir, Mr. Victor. Sure thing." He backed out of the room then turned, almost breaking into a run down the hallway.

"He's an odd duck." Ted surveyed the cart and poured himself a coffee.

"Yeah, and as loyal as they come." Victor poured a cup for Quinn and one for himself. "We crossed the threshold into hell in the days after Nam fell. I was deep in-country when the US bailed. Without his help, I never would have made it to the extraction point. I owe him my life."

"And vice versa since you brought him with you," Ted added. "Too many of the people who helped us got left behind."

Quinn sipped his coffee. He felt like an outsider in a place where he normally ruled like a king. "I didn't know that." He shook his head in an effort to chase fuzziness from his brain. "I'd forgotten you hired Chef." *Come to think of it, not long after Victor took charge, he replaced the whole staff. Even Mrs. Weaver is his.*

Ted opened a panel in the wall, next to the phone, revealing a sophisticated security system. He made a couple of entries and waited. A red light flashed, and the panel beeped. One of the wall monitors switched to a mosaic of live feeds from cameras around the mansion. "Mission control is live." Ted took a seat facing the monitor. "Victor? Do we have any idea who the Wolves of Karma are?"

"Not yet. But we will soon. I'll say one thing about them. They have some serious resources. And from Lester's description, they're brutal and efficient killers."

The security console buzzed. "That's Chef leaving the property." Ted motioned to the monitor showing a Prius zipping through the main gate. "We're clear."

Quinn returned to his conversation with Victor. "One

bullet in the head is efficient. Tearing people apart is psychotic and sadistic."

"You're thinking like a businessman. Think like a soldier. Fear is your greatest weapon. If your enemy fears you, your job is half done long before engagement. It's an ancient tactic, but effective."

"Okay, who are they scaring? Not you, apparently."

"I'm not the target." Victor's green eyes seemed to light from within. He was enjoying this.

Quinn could smell his own fear wafting off his damp body.

"Look around, Mr. Quinn. We have upped our alert level and locked down the mansion." He gestured with a half sandwich from the cart Chef had rolled in. "I've been thinking about the agenda behind this attack. Evidently, they don't want Queens developed, especially by Quinn Urban Development."

Quinn sipped his coffee. "Is that what you think?"

"So far, everyone who has died is connected with that project. I don't believe in coincidence. It has to be something along those lines."

"Why haven't they contacted me? At this point, I'd hear them out at least."

"They've spilled a lot of blood. The damage to you has been collateral—four men on the security staff, Grant, the banker, and your hacker." Victor took a bite of his sandwich and chewed thoughtfully. "Suppose they wanted you to build low-income housing on that block and turn it over to some local group to manage?"

"Over my dead body."

"Have you thought this through? They've bloodied the waters, but not enough to bend you to their will."

"What the hell are you trying to say, Victor? Spit it out, for Christ's sake."

"Is this block in Queens worth dying for?"

Quinn paused at the bluntness of the question. "Don't be ridiculous. It's a figure of speech."

"I'm not sure the Wolves of Karma have ruled out that eventuality. Is there anyone you're close to that I don't know about? A person who, if their life was threatened, could move you to do such a thing?"

Quinn shook his head. "No." He was very much alone. "Besides, it's not possible you wouldn't know—isn't it? If I'm not here, I'm in the car with Ted or at the office with Lester. You pretty much know where I am every minute of the day." A thought slowly formed in his mind. Victor had the knowledge and the means to conduct a sophisticated operation such as this. During the many hours they'd spent together over the last few years, Quinn had pieced together some interesting information about Victor. During his time in *The Service*, which Quinn had understood to be code for some black-ops branch of the CIA, Victor had overseen covert operations around the world as an in-country asset.

Quinn topped off his coffee. The events of the last twelve hours replayed in his mind and sharpened his assessment. It became increasingly clear how simple this would be for Victor to pull off. The only worm in the apple was motive. Victor was extremely well-compensated, as were Ted and Lester. If they wanted money, all they had to do was ask. None of them harbored humanitarian ideologies as far as Quinn knew. Of course, he only knew what little they told him aside from their official records, which were mostly works of fiction. Each of them had served in the military then gone on to college before ending up on a government payroll with some obscure title. Victor had alluded to his work with *The Service*. The other two never did, but Quinn knew the three of them had worked together.

His suspicions sharpened his mind further. He scrutinized every action and interaction between Ted and Victor, searching for any sign or attempt at manipulation. Tension in the room weighed heavily on his shoulders. Should he make an excuse to get out of there? *No. Keep your friends close and your enemies closer.*

The next half hour went by at a glacial pace. His mind spun up various scenarios, each one ending badly —for him.

"Something's up at the main gate." Ted operated the controls of the console until a close-up of the gate filled one flat screen. The camera slowly panned the area. There was no one there.

Victor moved closer to the screen. "Where the hell are they?"

Quinn lifted his sidearm.

Victor moved to the table and selected an assault rifle. Then he took a position next to the window.

"Check this shit out!" Ted pointed to the monitors as they went blank one at a time in rapid succession.

"Kill the lights in the residence." Victor palmed his phone and dialed.

"Who are you calling?" Quinn asked.

"Lester." Victor listened for a moment, thumbed the speaker, and held the phone out so Ted and Quinn could hear.

"You have reached the Wolves of Karma. If you have reached this number by mistake, hang up now and thank your creator. If not, prepare to meet Him." *Beeeeep.*

Victor spun on Ted. "Kill the fucking lights now."

"I did. Nothing's responding." Ted swung toward the door and positioned an assault rifle against his shoulder.

"Quinn, help me with this." Victor pushed the massive desk toward the door.

Alarms sounded on the security console. Ted glanced over. "Every zone is in alarm, even the second floor."

Quinn slammed the doors to the library closed and helped Victor move the desk into position against them. "Now what?"

His question was answered by the sound of smashing glass. All three windows imploded. The room detonated with rapid gunfire and the eerie snarl of wolves. When the slide locked open on Quinn's forty-five, Victor and Ted looked like two bags of bloody laundry. A half dozen snarling wolves encircled Quinn.

The desk was violently pushed into the room as the library doors burst open. Quinn looked around for a possible escape. There were none.

A tall figure stood in the doorway. He had long hair and a denim jacket. Hungry yellow eyes stared from a handsome face. "Good evening, Mr. Quinn. At last, we meet."

His heart raced, making it difficult to breathe. "Who are you? What do you want? Money? Name your price."

"We don't want your blood money."

"What, then? My life?" He edged a step toward one of the many weapons lying strewn around the room.

"No, Mr. Quinn. You have a greater penance to pay than these others." The man waved a hand casually over the tattered bodies of Ted and Victor. "They died doing *your* dirty work. They were more fortunate than you."

"What the fuck are we talking about here?" Quinn edged a little closer to the butt of an assault rifle. "Community service?"

Denim Jacket threw back his head in a snarling laugh.

Quinn inched a little farther.

"Yes, Mr. Quinn. Community service, of a sort, is exactly what we are talking about."

Quinn gauged his next move. "So spell it out."

Before Quinn could pivot and dive for the gun, Denim Jacket moved, picked up the weapon, and held it out to him. "Do you want this, Mr. Quinn?"

Quinn was startled by the inhuman speed. He hesitated with his hand partway extended.

"Have a seat, Mr. Quinn." With a hand, he nudged Quinn into a chair. "These are the Wolves of Karma. Allow me to introduce them to you. First, we have Mr. Sola."

The wolf on the far left raised his head.

"You may remember Mr. Sola as the warlord responsible for tens of thousands of senseless deaths in the Sudan."

"That's a wolf, trained maybe, but nothing more." Quinn pointed a finger at the standing figure. "And where is your makeup at tonight?"

In the blink of an eye, the handsome face transformed into that of a wolf. "Is this more to your liking? This was strictly theatrical." He held a hand up to his pointed snout. "For my own amusement. As to your associates, they all started life in the form of men but quickly turned into ruthless animals. I merely put an accurate face on them." His face returned to that of a man.

Quinn struggled with what he was seeing. "What has this to do with me?"

"We're getting to that." He motioned to the next beast. "Next, Mr. Amin, tyrant extraordinaire. There was much innocent suffering under his rule." He moved to the next. "Mr. Jones, the corporate executive responsible for countless deaths and suffering from polluting South America with mercury to expedite his mining interests."

Quinn exploded from his seat. "Who the fuck are you?"

"That is a more difficult question to answer. Think of me as an avenging angel."

"Avenging angel, my ass." Quinn pointed an accusing finger at the figure standing before him. "You're as brutal as the men you mentioned. You still haven't answered my question."

"It's quite simple. All these men increased the suffering of thousands of innocent lives to line their own useless pockets and, in some cases, for their own perverse pleasure. Their penance is to take the form of the brutal animals they were, go where I send them, and hurt men just like themselves. They enjoyed inflicting pain on the guileless, but I don't think they derive much pleasure from following my commands. Like them, you, Mr. Quinn, have also increased the pain and suffering of many people."

The icy fingers of dread clawed between his ribs and wrapped around his heart. "You have a lot of balls busting in here, accusing me. Look at the suffering you have caused this very night." He waved a hand at the bloody rags that had been Victor and Ted.

"I am not responsible for the men who died tonight. They suffered because of *you!* They are not innocents, far from it, but they need not have died the way they did."

"What if I change my ways?" Quinn pleaded. "Give me a chance to repent my sins."

The man smiled without humor. "This is no Charles Dickens novel. Our experience has shown that a leopard cannot change his spots."

"But there must be something I can do."

"There is indeed. You have been chosen to join the ranks of the Wolves of Karma. You are destined to spend eternity tearing out the throats of men much like yourself."

Quinn fell to his knees. He tilted his head back to beg for mercy. A long, mournful howl issued from his throat.

"There you are, Mr. Quinn. You make quite a striking wolf."

Thank you for reading Something's Amiss.
Still can't sleep?

Continue forth with a preview of his upcoming DROWNING IN
DARKNESS, a skin prickling tale of secrets co-written with D.
Browne.

Share your exciting discovery of a new read and help others add it to
their To Read lists by rating and/or writing a review on Goodreads
and Amazon.

Or you're welcome to stop in and visit Dave's website at:
http://www.davebenneman.com

Story One Marcus

The trip was a bad idea from the start. How had Marcus allowed his psychiatrist to talk him into this? The dread that had started at the airport escalated to full-blown terror as he turned the rental car onto Main Street.

Marcus wondered if he was the only thing that had changed in the past twenty years. The brick storefronts that lined the avenue gave Madison a quaint, small-town feel, and helped visitors ignore the potholes scattered in the road. A group of teenagers emerged from Zee's. The same pizza joint where Marcus had spent every Friday night. On game nights he'd never paid for a thing. The high school banner was faded and the "Z" in Zee's hung askew. He conceded something had changed after all.

Marcus had escaped Madison the summer after his graduation, returning only once to move his parents to Chicago. He stayed in touch with a few friends via Christmas Cards or social media. Cindy, his wife, thought the contact only aggravated his "condition". She had only agreed to this trip because Dr. Biggs recommended it. Yet, here he was. No one can run forever.

Vic's Bar and Grill approached on the right, the neon lights blinking in the afternoon light. Marcus had heard that Vic had taken over his old man's bar. Since Coach's funeral wasn't until 11:00 the next day and being alone with his thoughts in an empty hotel room did not appeal to him, Marcus decided to stop in for a drink.

He steered towards the bar in his cracker box rental. The first car the agency had offered him had more head-room, but it was… well, not acceptable, despite what his shrink might think of him. He pulled into the bar's parking lot and slid into a spot. Reaching to shut the car off, he noticed the mileage 007,228.3.

He froze as the car idled softly. It couldn't be. What were the odds? He could calculate them, but there was no need. It was an astronomical chance those five digits would align exactly like that. For the last few years, he had only bought cars that had over eight thousand miles and had sold them before they reached seventy thousand. At home, his car had a piece of tape discreetly placed over the odometer. Otherwise, he had found himself constantly staring at it while he drove. Not a safe driving technique, especially in Chicago.

The logical side of his brain justified all the reasons the numbers were meaningless. The odometer changed rapidly on a new car. Reaching seven thousand miles was no great feat.

Man, he needed a drink. He considered digging through his luggage for the medication his shrink prescribed. *Just turn it off and go inside. It's just a number.* His palms gathered sweat against the leather steering wheel, and the familiar heartburn bubbled up his throat.

It was no use. Three tenths of a mile, it's not likely he

would park with exactly three tenths on the odometer in this place, at this time. He backed the car out of the spot, drove around the block, and parallel parked a few doors down from the bar. He prayed Vic kept a decent scotch on hand.

Continue your journey with DROWNING IN DARKNESS, now available at Amazon.

Who is this guy?

Dave spent his formative years, front and center, watching horror movies on Saturday afternoons, and reading Edgar Allen Poe nightly before nodding off to sleep. He prefers mysteries about the dark nature of a world beyond what the naked eye can see.

When Dave is not traveling, he resides in Sunny Arizona with his wife and three furry companions.

f facebook.com/DaveBennemanAuthor

🐦 twitter.com/DaveBenneman

Made in the USA
San Bernardino, CA
25 March 2019